CONVERSATIONS

ON THE

ROAD

TO EMMAUS

CONVERSATIONS
ON THE
ROAD
TO EMMAUS

JESUS IN THE OLD TESTAMENT

Dr. John Mannion

AMBASSADOR INTERNATIONAL
GREENVILLE, SOUTH CAROLINA & BELFAST, NORTHERN IRELAND

www.ambassador-international.com

Conversations on the Road to Emmaus

Jesus in the Old Testament
©2022 by Dr. John Mannion
All rights reserved

ISBN: 978-1-64960-032-5
eISBN: 978-1-64960-033-2

Cover Design by Hannah Linder Designs
Interior Typesetting by Dentelle Design
Edited by Daphne Self

AMBASSADOR INTERNATIONAL
Emerald House
411 University Ridge, Suite B14
Greenville, SC 29601
United States
www.ambassador-international.com

AMBASSADOR BOOKS
The Mount
2 Woodstock Link
Belfast, BT6 8DD
Northern Ireland, United Kingdom
www.ambassadormedia.co.uk

The colophon is a trademark of Ambassador, a Christian publishing company.

To those who will walk on a future Road to Emmaus, my grandchildren:

John Carroll

Asaph Arturo

Rae Sawyer

Cavell Eliel

Cole Carroll

CONTENTS

PREFACE   11

INTRODUCTION   15

TORAH CONVERSATIONS (THE LAW) 23

CHAPTER 1
CONVERSING IN GENESIS   25

CHAPTER 2
CONVERSING IN EXODUS   51

CHAPTER 3
CONVERSING IN LEVITICUS, NUMBERS, DEUTERONOMY   61

NEVI'IM CONVERSATIONS (THE PROPHETS) 69

CHAPTER 4
CONVERSING IN JOSHUA, JUDGES   71

CHAPTER 5

CONVERSING IN SAMUEL, KINGS   77

CHAPTER 6

CONVERSING IN ISAIAH   83

CHAPTER 7

CONVERSING IN JEREMIAH, EZEKIEL   107

CHAPTER 8

CONVERSING IN HOSEA, JOEL, AMOS   113

CHAPTER 9

CONVERSING IN OBADIAH, JONAH,
MICAH, NAHUM   119

CHAPTER 10

CONVERSING IN HABAKKUK, ZEPHANIAH, HAGGAI   125

CHAPTER 11

CONVERSING IN ZECHARIAH, MALACHI   129

KETUVIM CONVERSATIONS (THE WRITINGS) . . . 141

CHAPTER 12

CONVERSING IN PSALMS   143

CHAPTER 13

CONVERSING IN PROVERBS, JOB,
SONG OF SONGS   161

CHAPTER 14

CONVERSING IN RUTH, LAMENTATIONS,
ECCLESIASTES 167

CHAPTER 15

CONVERSING IN ESTHER, DANIEL 171

CHAPTER 16

CONVERSING IN EZRA, NEHEMIAH, CHRONICLES 177

CONCLUSION 185

ABOUT THE AUTHOR 189

PREFACE

And behold, two of them were going that very day to a village named Emmaus, which was about seven miles from Jerusalem. And they were talking with each other about all these things which had taken place. While they were talking and discussing, Jesus Himself approached and *began* traveling with them. But their eyes were prevented from recognizing Him. And He said to them, "What are these words that you are exchanging with one another as you are walking?" And they stood still, looking sad. One *of them*, named Cleopas, answered and said to Him, "Are You the only one visiting Jerusalem and unaware of the things which have happened here in these days?" And He said to them, "What things?" And they said to Him, "The things about Jesus the Nazarene, who was a prophet mighty in deed and word in the sight of God and all the people, and how the chief priests and our rulers delivered Him to the sentence of death, and crucified Him. "But we were hoping that it was He who was going to redeem Israel. Indeed, besides all this, it is the third day since these things happened. But also some women among us amazed us. When they were at the tomb early in the morning, and did not find His body, they came, saying that they had also seen a vision of angels who said that He was alive. Some of those who were with us went to the tomb and found it just exactly as the women also had said; but Him they did not see." And He said to them, "O foolish men and slow of heart to believe in all that the prophets have spoken! Was it not necessary for the Christ to suffer these things and to enter into His glory?" Then beginning with Moses and with all the prophets, He explained to them the things concerning Himself in all the Scriptures. And they approached the village where they were going, and He acted as though He were going farther. But they urged Him, saying, "Stay with us, for it is getting toward evening, and the day is now nearly over." So He went in to stay with them. When He had reclined *at the table* with them, He took the bread and blessed *it*, and breaking *it*, He *began* giving *it* to them. Then their eyes were opened and they recognized Him; and He vanished from their sight. They said to one another, "Were not our hearts burning within us while He was speaking to us on the road, while He was explaining the Scriptures to us?" And they got up that very hour and returned to Jerusalem, and found gathered together the eleven and those who were with them, saying, "The Lord has really risen and has appeared to Simon." They *began* to relate their experiences on the road and how He was recognized by them in the breaking of the bread.[1]

It is understood that the canon is closed. There are no books to be deleted from the Bible and no new books to be added. Of course, I am not claiming that this book I have written is Scripture. I mention this because it may be seen as a bit of a fine line I am walking as I hypothesize what words Jesus used in a conversation about His appearances and activities in the Old Testament. Jesus, after He has been resurrected from the dead, is having an ongoing conversation with two disciples—who do not yet recognize Him—as He walks with them on the road to Emmaus. Since they do not yet recognize Him,[2] it is presumed that Jesus would have been speaking about Himself (referred to in this book as Jesus, the Christ, the Messiah, the Son of God, the Son of Man, the Son, or God) in the third person. One disciple is named Cleopas, and the other is left unnamed; and so, I have named him Jonathan. They engage in the conversation speaking in first person.

---

1   Luke 24:13-35, NASB
2   Mark 16:12

It is ultimately conjecture to say that Jesus actually said these exact words to two disciples while they walked together on the road to Emmaus. We do know, however, that He said something to them that was designed to explain how He is seen in the Old Testament. "Then beginning with Moses and with all the prophets, He explained to them the things concerning Himself in all the Scriptures."[1]

Having established my "disclaimer," I think that it can certainly be said that it is quite intriguing to propose what Jesus did say about Himself on that incredible day while on that incredible journey. It is not only intriguing, but it is also something—via interpretation of the Old Testament—that is not simply a guess with respect to what was actually discussed. Jesus is referencing the Old Testament. The Word is explaining the Word. Thus, this book is referencing the Old Testament (referred to as the Scriptures, the ancient Scriptures, the Old Covenant, or the Hebrew-derived Tanakh) as it hypothesizes how the Word actually explained the Word. Of course, it is understood that there is interpretation involved here, and thus, there is room for error. Nevertheless, I believe that it can confidently be said that the content of this book is consistent with the content of Scripture, and thus, a fascinating thing to examine—*CONVERSATIONS ON THE ROAD TO EMMAUS!*

*Note: It is understood that Jesus would not refer to the Scriptures with chapter and verse. They did not exist in that form at that time (they were inserted in the mid-sixteenth century). Nevertheless, for the sake of clear documentation, I will cite passages—both Old and New Testament—with a book, chapter, and verse reference via a system of endnotes. This method of referencing depicts the nature of this book—a "novel" (method of writing) combined with a "Bible commentary" (content of writing). Thus, this "non-fiction novel" comes with conversation along with biblical interpretation, explanation, and referencing.

---

1   Luke 24:27

Herein, lies the unique nature of this work as it covers this particular topic. It very much reads like a novel, informal and engaging in that sense. At the same time, it fills the reader with the fruit of a detailed Bible commentary. This unique, non-fiction story, then, is both enjoyable and enlightening to read. So, let us walk together as we engage in *Conversations on the Road to Emmaus*!

John Mannion

INTRODUCTION

The most significant question Jesus asks is, "Who do you say that I am?"[1] Who is Jesus? Some people like to say that He was a great teacher so as to show Him respect without having to enter into the more controversial discussion. Maybe He was a prophet. Maybe He was a great revolutionary standing up for moral and social causes Who ultimately would inspire people to take a stand for social justice.

As much as all these descriptions of Jesus are consistent with what He did, they are not fully correct with respect to Who He actually is, since Who He actually is cannot simply be satisfied by any of those descriptions.

One who is simply a teacher does not say, "Jerusalem, Jerusalem, who kills the prophets and stones those who are sent to her! How often I wanted to gather your children together, the way a hen gathers her chicks under her wings, and you were unwilling."[2] Who is this? He claims that He often wanted to gather together the inhabitants of a city under His wings!

One who is simply a prophet does not say, "I am the way, and the truth, and the life; no one comes to the Father but through Me."[3] Who is this? He claims that He *is* the life and the *only* way to God!

One who is simply a revolutionary does not say, "Truly, truly, I say to you, before Abraham was born, I am."[4] Who is this? He claims that He existed before a man who lived two thousand years before Him.

---

1   Matthew 16:15
2   Matthew 23:37
3   John 14:6
4   John 8:58

15

Who is this? Aha, now we get to that "more controversial discussion." You either have to say He is God, or you have to say He is a liar and/or a lunatic. But you cannot just say He was a great Teacher. He does not claim to just be a great Teacher. No. He claims over and over again in a variety of ways not to be a liar or a lunatic, but to be Lord!

Who is Jesus? He is God!

Knowing Who Jesus really is, who would not give all he had to have walked with Him when He was on this earth? Who would not have loved to have been there when He multiplied the bread or when He walked on water? Who would not give all to see all the things that happened from His virgin birth to His resurrection from the dead? More specifically, what would one give to sit in on one of those actual "conversations" we only get a glimpse of in the Scriptures? I certainly would love to have sat in on the conversation in the boat after the feeding of the four thousand.[5] How about the conversation with His disciples after Peter's revelation of Him as the Christ and the ensuing warning not to tell others yet?[6] Oh, how incredible it would have been to be privy to the conversation between Jesus, Moses, and Elijah at the transfiguration.[7] What was included in the likely conversation among the disciples after Jesus told them of His ensuing death?[8] How curious with regard to an even more specific kind of scene, for example, in which the disciples went to the Mount of Olives "after singing a hymn."[9] What kind of hymn was it? What did it sound like? How long was it, and what were the words? And, yes, talk about curious! How did the two women report the resurrection to Jesus' disciples?[10] What did they say? What kind of emotional presentation was attached to those words? With what level of conviction did they speak? Maybe one of the most desirable events to have been a part of would have been when Jesus "was teaching daily in the temple."[11] Oh, to have sat in on a class with Professor Jesus!

---

5   Matthew 15:39
6   Matthew 16:20
7   Matthew 17:3
8   Matthew 17:22-23
9   Matthew 26:30
10 Matthew 28:8
11 Luke 19:47

Perhaps, the ultimate conversation to have access to, however, is one that we actually can, with some degree of accuracy, replicate—the conversation between Jesus and two of His disciples on the road to Emmaus.[12] What a conversation! As they walked on the road together, Jesus began with Moses (the Law or the Pentateuch) and explained to these two very blessed individuals all the things concerning Himself in all the Scriptures.[13] The two disciples tried to explain to others this wondrous thing that had happened to them but could only say that Jesus had explained the Scriptures to them.[14] What were "the Scriptures?" Jesus clearly and explicitly answered that question when He said, "These are My words which I spoke to you while I was still with you, that all things which are written about Me in ***the Law of Moses and the Prophets and the Psalms*** must be fulfilled. Then He opened their minds to understand the Scriptures."[15] (author's emphasis) For Jesus, the "Scriptures" would have been what Christians now call the Old Testament and what Jews call the Masoretic text or the Tanakh. *TaNaKh* is an acronym using the first Hebrew letter of each of the Masoretic text's three traditional subdivisions: Torah ("Law," also known as the Five Books of Moses or the Pentateuch); Nevi'im ("Prophets," which consists of the "Former Prophets," the "Major Prophets," and the "Minor Prophets"); and Ketuvim ("Writings," which are represented by the Psalms and include wisdom, history, and poetry books like Proverbs, Ecclesiastes, and Song of Songs). Hence, we have the acronym *TaNaKh* (Jesus may have referred to the Tanakh as the Mikra, meaning "reading" or "that which is read").

The modern-day Jewish Tanakh is the same as the modern-day Christian Old Testament. The only differences are that some books in the Tanakh are combined like Samuel, Kings, and Chronicles; and some books are placed in a different order (for example, Chronicles being at the end of the Tanakh instead of being placed soon after the books of the Law, as in the Old Testament).

---

12   Luke 24:13-35
13   Luke 24:27
14   Luke 24:32
15   Luke 24:44-45

The thirty-nine books of the Old Testament would have been Jesus' Bible or Scriptures. It is from these books that Jesus "explained to them the things concerning Himself in all the Scriptures."[16]

Thus, *Conversations on the Road to Emmaus* will be organized according to these divisions of the Old Testament or Tanakh. Jesus will first converse through the "Law," then through the "Prophets," and finally, through the "Writings." Every book is represented in these conversations, since He is seen *in* every book. Thus, the specific order of conversation will reflect the specific order of the Tanakh as follows:

The Law

- Genesis
- Exodus
- Leviticus
- Numbers
- Deuteronomy

The Prophets

- Joshua
- Judges
- Samuel
- Kings
- Isaiah
- Jeremiah
- Ezekiel
- Hosea
- Joel
- Amos
- Obadiah
- Jonah
- Micah
- Nahum
- Habakkuk
- Zephaniah
- Haggai
- Zechariah
- Malachi

The Writings

- Psalms
- Proverbs
- Job
- Song of Songs
- Ruth
- Lamentations
- Ecclesiastes
- Esther
- Daniel
- Ezra
- Nehemiah
- Chronicles

While we may only be able to hypothesize about the other conversations mentioned earlier, we have more of a foundation to project from when it comes to the conversations on the road to Emmaus.

Jesus is the Word of God; thus, He is the Tanakh and can easily and readily be seen in it. Furthermore, the revealing of Jesus is the very purpose of the Tanakh. This is made obvious when Jesus rebukes the Jews for seeking to use the Tanakh for other purposes: "You search the Scriptures because you think that in them you have eternal life; it is these that testify about Me . . . For if you believed Moses, you would believe Me, for he wrote about Me."[17] Here we have, perhaps, the most emphatically ironic piece of theology ever expressed as Jesus basically says, "You search the Scriptures, and here I am; . . . in all your searching, you look right past me!" Another way to hear the irony is to picture Jesus saying, "You search through the Scriptures, but you don't see the Scriptures, even though the Scriptures are standing right in front of you." It is not theologically incorrect to hear Jesus saying, "I am the Word. I am the Scriptures. Search Me, and you search them."

My first seminary course was Old Testament Survey. In the course introduction, my professor told us a very profound thing. He said, "When you read the Old Testament, look for Jesus, and it comes alive!" The Old Testament can be fully understood only when we read it through the lens of the Person of Christ, just as the Old Covenant is better understood in light of the New Covenant. Indeed, "so much the more Jesus has become the guarantee of a better covenant."[18] This is not a totally different covenant, but a more complete and more clearly revealed covenant, even as Jesus the Lamb of God is the more complete and more clearly revealed method of enacting that covenant. "The next day he saw Jesus coming to him and said, 'Behold, the Lamb of God who takes away the sin of the world!'"[19]

---

17 John 5:39, 46
18 Hebrews 7:22
19 John 1:29-30

There is no different Divine method here for salvation. People were saved in the Old Covenant the same way they are now saved under the New Covenant. They are saved by God's provision of a sacrifice that would serve as a substitution or replacement for the sinner who would, in turn, accept and have faith in God's provision. The lamb in the Old Covenant is less of a revelation than the Lamb in the New Covenant. The Lamb in the New Covenant is "better"—not because there is a different God or method of God in the Old Covenant but because there is a more direct, clear, and complete revelation of God and His salvific method in the New Covenant.[20]

There is not one God in the Old Covenant and another God in the New Covenant. There is only one God. The Jews knew this, and even the demons know this.[21] When Jesus explains Himself in all of the Old Testament, He forever declares what is already known—He is God who never changes. "Jesus Christ is the same yesterday and today and forever."[22] He is seen in the Old Testament because Who He is in the New Testament is seen in the Old Testament. There is no different God, just a different degree of the revelation of that God.

Conversations on the Road to Emmaus very much stands as a rejection of any type of "two Gods theology" (a God of the Old Testament and another God of the New Testament) and/or any type of "two salvations theology" (one way to get saved in the Old Testament and a completely other way to get saved in the New Testament). Jesus and His Gospel are the same "yesterday, and today, and forever." He does not change. From Old to New Covenant, He is the same God with the same plan of salvation embodied in a clearer, fuller, and more complete revelation of that same God Who has that same plan of salvation. The New Covenant does not change God and His plan of salvation; it just continues and perfects/fulfills the revelation of it. God is not Judge/holy in the Old Testament and Savior/loving in the New Testament. God is always

---

20 Hebrews 8-10
21 Deuteronomy 6:4; James 2:19
22 Hebrews 13:8

Judge and Savior, holy and loving. He does not start being loving and stop being holy in the New Testament. He is not in process. God is not One Who matures. He is forever perfect. He does not change. The degree to which He reveals Himself changes.

And so, it is with these understandings that we begin our walk with great expectation. Of course, Jesus is *seen* in the Old Testament. He *is* the Old Testament!

TORAH
CONVERSATIONS
(THE LAW)

CHAPTER 1
CONVERSING IN GENESIS

He is risen! He is risen, indeed!

Early that morning, some of the women who were followers of Jesus went to the tomb where He was buried. He was not there. Two men in dazzling clothing suddenly appeared and proclaimed, "He is risen!"

Later, two of His disciples were walking on the road to Emmaus discussing all these things.

"I really hoped that He was the One," Cleopas said with a sense of profound disappointment.

"Yes, it is hard to make sense of it all," Jonathan agreed. "Unless, the women who went to the tomb early this morning were seeing things clearly, there is no hope. In fact, if He is not raised from the dead, then our faith is in vain; and we are of all men most to be pitied."[1]

Jesus approached the two men and began to walk with them, but they did not recognize Him. "What are you discussing?" Jesus inquired.

"What are we discussing? Are you the only one in Jerusalem who does not know about the things that have happened here in the last three days?" Cleopas waited for an answer.

"The things about Jesus of Nazareth," Jonathan added. "How He was a prophet mighty in word and deed but was nailed to a cross by the rulers."

"Yes, and now it is the third day," Cleopas mournfully whispered.

---

1   Matthew 28:1-8; 1 Corinthians 15:12-19

"We were hoping He was the One who would redeem Israel. We don't know what to think. There were some women among us who went to the tomb early this morning and reported that He was not there and that angels told them that He is risen." Jonathan contributed these words with a tone of hope laced with confusion and fear.

Jesus responded with a tone of clarity and assurance. "Was it not necessary for the Christ to suffer these things and to enter into His glory?" Then he began with Moses and the prophets, and explained to them all that had ever been foretold about Himself.[2]

Jonathan stared at Him quizzically. "I do not know Who You are, but I perceive you are a prophet and a teacher. Please walk with us and teach us these things about the Christ in the Scriptures."

And so, Jesus walked with them and engaged in conversations on the road to Emmaus.

"The Christ, the Messiah, the Son of God—this One you called Jesus— is seen in the Law, the Prophets, and the Writings—the Torah, the Nevi'im, and the Ketuvim. This is what is called the Tanakh, the Scriptures. Of course, the best place to begin in these ancient Scriptures is in the beginning—in Genesis, the book of beginnings."

"How is the Messiah seen in Genesis?" Cleopas asked sincerely. "Is the Son of God actually involved in the Creation? What does our religion say?"

"Well, of course, the Son of God is in the beginning, for 'in the beginning God created,'" Jesus said matter-of-factly. "The meaning of the term 'religion' is rooted in the quest to understand what everything is tied back to. What is the beginning? Is it the Creation? Perhaps, it is some sort of colossal bang? No! It is not the creation. It is the Creator. The Creator, of course, created. What did He create out of? It is not so much that He created out of nothing for then 'nothing' would have had to itself, at some point, been created lest it be understood as being eternal, and thus, divine."

Jonathan exclaimed, "Ahh yes! This is what the people from the East call nirvana."

Jesus continued, "You see, 'nothing' is not Divine. It is not some sort of primordial eternal ooze from which all creation came into being; nor is it a 'pre-creation substance' that God made and then used to fashion 'the heavens and the earth.' If God used any 'substance'—whether that substance be that which is or that which is not—from which to fashion any other substance, then that original substance would have to have been, itself, created. Do not miss the point here! The only way a Creator can be a Creator is that He is eternal. That is the most foundational definition of the Creator; He is the Eternal One. So, too, that is the most foundational definition of the Eternal One—the One Who has no beginning, the One Who everything else goes back to; He is the Creator. He never began. For at some point, all that began finds its way back to something else that never began. Of course, that is the beginning!"

Jonathan coughed and then asked, "Yes, but what did that come from?"

"It came from something that came before it," Jesus responded as if He were meditating on that fact. "And what came before that? If it is 'nothing' and there is nothing that came before 'nothing,' then 'nothing,' is eternal and is, therefore, God. Then the followers of the Eastern religions would be correct. However, if 'nothing' is not what everything else came from, then everything else came from something. Ultimately, whatever stands as that 'last' something else is, of course, God, since it is, of course, eternal. It is self-existing. It has no beginning and no end. If that which had made something else, or caused something else, or led to something else actually had a beginning, then it would have had to have had a 'beginner' and would not then, by definition, be God."

"Then how did everything start?" Cleopas asked almost impatiently.

Jesus responded, "It started with the only thing it could have started with—the Starter Who had no start. He is God. And so, it is not surprising to understand that there is a substance or a being from which all else was created. That beginning 'material' is nothing less than the Beginner Himself. This, of course, does not mean that creation is Divine. No, creation is separate from the Creator, even as the pot is separate from the potter. If the creation were Divine, then it would not be creation at all. Yes, creation is, indeed, created. It is not the Creator. It is not God. It is, however, created through God.

"Jesus continued, 'For by Him all things were created, *both* in the heavens and on earth, visible and invisible, whether thrones or dominions or rulers or authorities—all things have been created through Him and for Him. He is before all things, and in Him all things hold together.'[3] In the beginning God the Father 'created the heavens and the earth.'[4] In the same way, 'In the beginning was the Word, and the Word was with God, and the Word was God. He was in the beginning with God. All things came into being through Him, and apart from Him nothing came into being that has come into being.'[5] And so, with regard to the Son of God who is the Word of God, it is 'by Him,' 'through Him,' and 'for Him' that creation was accomplished."

Cleopas stumbled and nearly fell down on the road. "This is an incredible statement about the Christ, the Son of God!"

"Creation was not made out of, or through, nothing. It was made out of, or through, Him," Jesus explained. "The Messiah is seen in the Scriptures in the first five words of Scripture: 'In the beginning God created . . . .' He is seen before the beginning. When was that? It was not just 'before that.' No, it was in the 'realm of the never began.' It was in the realm where, when, and how only God exists. The eternal Son of God is seen in the first words of Scripture. Nevertheless, man cannot comprehend it even as the one who is created cannot, ultimately, grasp the One who created him since the one who began cannot, ultimately, go back to the 'realm of no beginning.'[6] Perhaps

---

3   Colossians 1:16-17
4   Genesis 1:1
5   John 1:1-3
6   Ecclesiastes 3:11; Job 37:5

this is why the one who is religious—the one who tries to 'tie things back'—sometimes becomes frustrated with his inability to completely understand, and thus sometimes does not live by faith, but instead, lives by hypocrisy."[7]

Jesus stopped and bent down, drawing something in the dirt on the side of the road. Looking up at Cleopas and Jonathan, He said, "Again, do not miss the point. You cannot insist on traveling back to the realm of no beginning. You cannot insist on being God, for then your religion brings you back to the Garden of Eden and the toxic tree that you foolishly think will triumphantly escort you to the realm of no beginning, to the realm of the Definer[8] or the realm of the eternal. You cannot be God. Allow your God to be God. Allow Him to take you back to the Tree of Life in the garden as He performs the greatest act of creation of all time.[9] His own substitutionary death reverses your death and grants you new life. Indeed, you can become a new creation.[10] You can shake off the frustrating chains of religion and put on the life giving robe of Christ."[11]

Again, Jesus stopped and bent down, drawing something in the dirt on the side of the road. Looking up at Cleopas and Jonathan, He said, "Do not miss the point. As the Christ said, 'This is eternal life, that they may know You, the only true God, and Jesus Christ whom You have sent.'[12] You can never fully comprehend eternity, but you can live there. This mystery is great.[13] You can never be God, but you can live with Him. You can live with Him—you can live in eternity—through knowing Christ. And so, Christ is seen in the ancient Scriptures as long as you don't miss the point."

"And so, the Christ, in a very real sense, is active as the Creator. He *is* the beginning!" It was not totally clear whether Jonathan was making a conclusive statement or asking a contending question.

---

7   Galatians 2:20; Matthew 23:28
8   Genesis 3:5
9   Revelation 2:7
10   Galatians 6:15; John 3:3, 7
11   Luke 15:22
12   John 17:3
13   Ephesians 5:32

Jesus paused, looked him in the eye, and said, "Christ is the Alpha and Omega, the beginning and the end, who was, who is, and who will be.[14] Light was created[15] because Christ was. Light of revelation leads men now[16] because Christ is. Light shall shine on the new Jerusalem[17] because Christ will be."

As they continued walking down the road, Jesus explained the holiness of Christ as seen in the creation. "His holiness—His separation—is seen in that 'God separated the light from the darkness.'[18] The world was made through Christ. He is the Light. Thus, the light was separated from the darkness; it was made holy. Christ's holiness is seen in the Tanakh."

"Teacher, these things are hard to understand," mumbled Cleopas.

Jonathan changed the energy of the moment as he lifted up an excited request. "Teacher, show us more of the Christ in the creation."

"Christ is the Creator. The Father, the Son, and the Holy Spirit—the Trinity—is the only Creator. All was made through the Son.[19] He is God. A 'process' is not God. A 'process' did not create. God—not God's process—created every living thing. Just as it is now, it was when God created it. He made the beasts of the Earth after their kind.[20] Christ is seen in the Scriptures as the Creator."

"The Son of God is God," proclaimed Jonathan.

"And God is One,[21] yet in three Persons,"[22] added Cleopas.

"Herein, we see the Son of God again in the creation," Jesus explained. "Man was created to reflect his Creator. 'God created man in His own image, in the image of God He created him; male and female He created them.'[23] When God created man, He did not create him as a horse. He did not create him as

---

14   Revelation 1:8
15   Genesis 1:3; John 1:4-10
16   2 Corinthians 4:6; Luke 2:32
17   Revelation 21:23-24
18   Genesis 1:4
19   John 1:10
20   Genesis 1:11-25; Genesis 6:20
21   Deuteronomy 6:4
22   2 Corinthians 13:14; Matthew 28:19
23   Genesis 1:27

a plant or as a cockroach. He did not create him as a fish or a pig which has no soul or spirit. He created him in His image. This is why you, Cleopas, do not look like a horse nor you, Jonathan, look like a plant or a cockroach or a fish or a pig. The incarnate Christ, in Whose image you were made, was 'made in the likeness of men,'[24] even as man was made in the image of God. The singular, triune God made mankind male and female (a singular plurality). The triune God, Who is One, is a singular plurality, even as mankind, who is made in His image, is a singular plurality. God, Who is a compound unity and not a singular non-diverse unity, is an *Us* Who makes a *Them*[25] Who shall become *one*.[26] Jesus is seen in the Tanakh."

Jonathan stopped suddenly and said, "Let's go over to the side of the road here and rest for a little while."

The three men sat down on a large rock and took off their sandals. "It is so nice to be able to rest." Cleopas sighed. "Even God rested on the seventh day!"[27]

"Truly, it is in the Sabbath that Christ is seen once again in the events of the creation," Jesus remarked. "The Son of Man, the Christ, is Lord of the Sabbath,[28] even as He 'blessed the seventh day and sanctified it.'[29] He who blesses it and sanctifies it is, indeed, Lord over it. Hence, Jesus is seen once again in the Tanakh."

Jesus, seemingly playing in the dirt, began to form out of the mud a tiny figure that looked like a man. "What have I just done with this dirt, Jonathan?"

"You have taken the position of God and have created something that resembles a type of man."

"Ah, yes, a 'type.' Christ can sometimes be seen in the Scriptures by means of someone or something that is a 'type' of Him or His actions. A 'type' is

---

24 Philippians 2:7
25 Genesis 1:26
26 Genesis 2:24
27 Genesis 2:2
28 Luke 6:5
29 Genesis 2:3

a historical fact that illustrates or points to a spiritual truth. For example, Adam is a type of Christ,[30] even as Adam entered the world as a sinless man through a special act of God[31] and became the head of the old creation—the first Adam. Christ entered the world as a sinless Man through a special act of God[32] and became the Head of the new creation—the last Adam.[33] Through Adam as a type of Christ, we see Jesus in the Tanakh.

"Cleopas and Jonathan, look at those trees across the road. What do you see?"

"I see two trees," answered Cleopas. "Is that supposed to mean something? Hey, Jonathan. Do you see anything else?"

"I see two trees . . . in the garden."

"Yes, Jonathan," Jesus exclaimed. "You have eyes that see! Jesus is 'the way, and the truth, and the life.'[34] He is the Tree of Life in the garden; He is the Life. He is the Tree of the Knowledge of Good and Evil in the garden; He is the Way and the Truth.[35] Jesus, in the two trees in the garden, is seen in the Tanakh."

"We should begin our journey again," Cleopas suggested with a clear sense of reluctance. "It sure is tempting to just sit here and rest."

Jonathan chimed in immediately. "Yes, but we must not fall to the temptation."

Jesus added, "Like Adam and Eve fell to temptation in the garden?"

"May God help us!" cried Jonathan.

"Yes, but even in the temptation in the garden, Christ can be seen," Jesus added as He got up off the rock and began to walk down the road again. "Adam was confronted with three temptations and failed. Christ was confronted with the same three temptations and did not fail. You see, all temptation is wrapped up in three sorts; 'all that is in the world, the lust of the flesh and the

---

30 Romans 5:14
31 Genesis 2:7
32 Luke 1:34-35
33 1 Corinthians 15:45
34 John 14:6
35 Genesis 2:9

lust of the eyes and the boastful pride of life.'[36] For Adam, 'the tree was good for food'; the lust of the flesh. It was a 'delight to the eyes'; the lust of the eyes. And it was 'desirable to make one wise'; the boastful pride of life.[37] Christ, in a very real sense, was there in the garden as He would go through the same temptations, yet without sinning.[38] Jesus was tempted[39] with the suggestion, 'turn these stones to bread'; lust of the flesh. Then He was offered 'all the kingdoms of the world'—the lust of the eyes. Finally, He was challenged to show off by throwing Himself off a cliff and not getting hurt—the boastful pride of life. And so, in the temptations in the garden, Christ is seen as He turns defeat into victory."

"Cleopas," Jesus entreated, almost as if He was taking attendance in His classroom.

"Yes, Teacher?" Cleopas replied appropriately.

"What did you see on Friday that turned your own defeat into victory; that turned your own condemnation into forgiveness?"

Jonathan interrupted, "Without the shedding of blood there is no forgiveness of sins."[40]

"Are we talking about the blood Christ shed on the cross up on that God forsaken hill three days ago?" inquired Cleopas with a tone of discontent."

"Indeed, we are," confirmed Jesus. "Thankfully, however, it is the exact opposite of 'God forsaken.' In fact, Cleopas, without that miraculous intervention of God in which He sent His only begotten Son, the Christ, to come into this world as a Man and die on a cross for the payment of your sins, you would have no hope."

Jonathan took a long step forward to stand in front of Jesus. Face to face, he inquired, "How early on in the Tanakh is this hope seen? Is the Christ seen in this way even in the book of beginnings?"

---

36   1 John 2:16
37   Genesis 3:6
38   1 John 3:5; 2 Corinthians 5:21; Hebrews 4:15
39   Luke 4:1-13
40   Hebrews 9:22

"Aha, Jonathan, you are starting to get it! The Christ is seen right away in the Scriptures, even with regard to this great mystery—this mystery in which God becomes a Man and spills His blood on a tree to win the war against the ultimate opponent, Satan. And so, in the garden, after Satan successfully tempted Adam and Eve and they sinned against God, God passes judgment on Satan, saying, 'And I will put enmity between you and the woman, and between your seed and her seed; He shall bruise you on the head, and you shall bruise him on the heel.'"[41]

"What is 'enmity'?" pondered Jonathan.

"Stop and look," Jesus requested. "What do you see? It is a man chopping off the head of a chicken as he prepares for the day's meal. That, Jonathan, is enmity. It is a blood feud!"

Cleopas somewhat reluctantly entered the discussion, "And so the blood feud is between Satan specifically, or evil in general, and Eve specifically, or fallen humanity in general?"

Jesus veered off a bit toward the side of the road and the two disciples followed. He picked up two seeds lying next to a small plant. "The prophecy asserts that there are two seeds that stand against each other—the evil seed on the one hand and the seed of the woman on the other hand."

"Who is that seed of the woman?" Cleopas probed.

"The seed of the woman is the incarnate Christ.[42] The Son of God becomes a Man so as to fight on behalf of mankind in the blood feud with Satan. He will use His own blood to win the war and to win salvation for mankind. He will crush Satan's head and destroy him while Satan will bruise Him on the heel, yet He will not be destroyed but will be risen."

"We indeed saw this on Friday," both Jonathan and Cleopas exclaimed at the same time. "The soldiers drove the spikes into His heel as His blood dripped down the cross."

41 Genesis 3:15
42 Galatians 3:16

"Yes, and now it is Sunday, and you shall see the glory of God. What did the women who went to the tomb early this morning say to you? Did they not proclaim, 'He is risen from the dead'? He was not destroyed and defeated. He was only injured in the heel and will show His victory in the resurrection."

"Cleopas," Jonathan rejoiced. "Did we not begin this journey with a hope in our hearts the women were right? That He is risen from the dead? And now this prophet, this Teacher Who walks with us, has shown us these things as they are pictured first thing in the ancient Scriptures. Brother, we have hope, do we not?"

Cleopas stopped and stared down at the ground. He kicked a clump of dirt and sighed. "I want to hope, Jonathan. After all that has happened these past three days, however, I just don't know what to think. I just don't know. In any case, let's press on toward Emmaus."

Jesus suggested, "Come, my friends, let us first sit for a moment under this cedar tree. I want to talk to you concerning a sensitive topic. God's provision of blood for the forgiveness of sins is seen after the fall of man in the garden even with respect to the realm of the sexual. It is the sin of man that corrupts that which is sexual. However, it was not always this way. In fact, before sin came into the world, there was no shame or awkwardness in the sexual relationship between the husband and the wife. They became 'one flesh,' and they were naked and not ashamed.[43] After the Fall, there was shame and awkwardness in the sexual realm. So, they tried to hide their nakedness.[44]

"Man always tries to hide his own nakedness by his own efforts, but to no avail.[45] Only Christ can provide this covering for sin.[46] And so, God makes garments of skin for the man and the woman, shedding blood to do so, and provides a covering for their sin.[47] He clothes them with the forgiveness that comes from the shedding of blood,[48] albeit within the context of sin.[49] Herein,

43 Genesis 2:24-25
44 Genesis 3:7
45 Ephesians 2:8-9
46 Galatians 2:21
47 Genesis 3:21
48 Hebrews 9:22
49 Romans 5:8

the Christ and His shed blood on the cross for salvation, are seen early on in the Tanakh."

As they sat under the cedar tree, Jesus began to arrange some sticks in a certain way. Three sticks lay evenly separated from each other forming a sort of circle. One other stick was stuck into the ground as it stood in the middle of the circle of three sticks.

"What is that you are depicting with those sticks?" probed Cleopas with a sense of expectation.

Jonathan offered, "It seems to be a picture of something that is three-in-one. Perhaps the Teacher is portraying the nature of God as a sort of Trinity. The Shema tells us that God is One.[50] Yet, we know He exists in three Persons: Father, Son, and Holy Spirit."[51]

"Yes, my brothers," Jesus responded. "These sticks represent the nature of God as a Trinity; and the Trinity is, indeed, seen in a variety of ways in the very beginnings of the Law. In fact, the Trinity is seen in the very first sentences of the Scriptures. The Father created through the Son and by the Holy Spirit.[52] Furthermore, God is often referenced as a singular plurality.[53] He is 'El'—singular God—'ohim'—plural ending. This plural noun is attached to a singular verb—not because of incorrect grammar but because of correct theology. Thus, it is not surprising that God speaks as an 'Us' Who is an 'Our.'[54] Finally, in these earliest writings in the Law, we see the singular plurality of the Trinity in the divine institution of marriage[55] as Elohim created man in His own image—His own singular, plurality image—by creating *him* 'male and female he created *them*.'"[56]

Cleopas struggled to summarize his thoughts. "Are we to understand then that a 'Them' creates a 'them,' making the marriage the holiest institution

50 Deuteronomy 6:4
51 Matthew 28:19
52 Genesis 1:1-2; Colossians 1:16
53 Genesis 1-3
54 Genesis 1 26; Genesis 3:22
55 Genesis 1 27
56 Genesis 5:2

of mankind[57] even as its 'singular plurality' is a direct reflection of the very nature of God?"

Jesus collected the sticks and threw them into the brush. "This mystery is great.[58] God, Who is a singular plurality, creates in His image a singular plurality—a 'They' Who become 'one.'[59] Indeed, the Christ, in the Trinity, is seen in the Scriptures. Let's walk onward," He suggested.

"It is important that we keep moving," Jonathan agreed.

"Yes, Jonathan, it is important." Jesus paused. "What is the most important message in the Scriptures?"

"The Good News," answered Jonathan confidently. "Yes, the Gospel message!"

"You are correct, my friend. Throughout the Scriptures, this Good News is proclaimed. Man is unable, but God is able. Man needs, and God provides. Man is lost, but God finds him. Man cannot get to God, so God comes to man. Man cannot pay for his own forgiveness, so God pays the price for him. Man cannot save himself by his own works, so God saves man by His work on the cross—by His own shed blood. This is the Good News. This is the Gospel message."

Jonathan turned to Cleopas. "Is not your heart burning within you?"

"Who is this Man?" Cleopas repeated the question almost as if he was trying to express a mix of anger and jubilation. "Who is this Man?"

Jesus, meanwhile, was walking a few strides ahead of them. He turned to face them while still walking backwards. "The Gospel message is seen in a variety of ways early on in the Law. Not long after Adam and Eve leave the Garden of Eden, the blood that is needed by man as proclaimed by the Gospel message is provided by God. This prefigures the ultimate provision of God— Christ's blood on the cross. It also prefigures man's rejection of the provision of God or man's acceptance of that provision.

---

57   Genesis 2:18
58   Ephesians 5:31-32
59   Genesis 2:22-23

Jesus paused and looked straight into the eyes of Cleopas. "Why, when I was proclaiming the Good News of the Gospel, did you react with both anger and jubilation? Might you have in you a little bit of Cain and a little bit of Abel? Remember, my friend, if you do well, you will only have jubilation; but if you do not do well, sin is crouching at the door."[60]

Jesus then continued His discourse. "Man's rejection of the provision of God is seen in the good works theology of Cain, who tries to offer to God a non-blood offering, an 'I can do it' offering based on works. This is not good news. This is bad news because Cain's own work could never earn him forgiveness. Man's acceptance of the provision of God is seen in the substitutionary theology of Abel, who offers to God a blood offering, an 'I cannot do it' offering based on God's provision.[61] This is good news. This is good news because Abel's reliance, trust, and faith in God can result in forgiveness and salvation for him."

Jesus paused as if to let the two men soak in all that He had just said. "Who are you, Jonathan? A son of Abel or a son of Cain? Who are you, Cleopas? A son of Abel or a son of Cain? What do you rely on? Your own good works or the substitutionary death of Christ on the cross? Is the blood of Christ that is seen in Abel's offering a stumbling block to you, or is it good news?"

Jonathan and Cleopas walked on in silence. Their hearts were burning within them. At the same time, their heads were almost unable to process all that they were hearing. The Teacher was only in the very first sections of the Law, and already He had shown them Christ in the Scriptures in so many ways.

Both men kept mumbling under their breath, 'Who is this?'"

Finally, Jesus broke the silence. "We are walking on the road to Emmaus. Just think if you could walk on the road to eternity!"

"I know of no road to eternity," argued Cleopas. "How am I to walk on it? Where is it?"

---

60 Genesis 4:5-7
61 Genesis 4:3-5

"The walk itself is where eternity is," Jesus explained. "Eternal life is to know Jesus.[62] It is to walk with Him even as 'Enoch walked with God; and he was not, for God took him.'[63] Enoch pointed to Christ as he walked with Him right into eternity." Herein, Jesus is seen in the Tanakh."

"Yes, the great men of old display Christ in the Tanakh," Jesus continued. "Adam, Able, Enoch, and Noah. Christ is the Ark of salvation. When Noah, by faith, stepped into that ark and was saved,[64] he did nothing less than enter the ark of Jesus' salvation.[65]

"The paradox of the Trinity, and therefore the Person of Christ, shows up all over the place in the Scriptures. Just as God is with Himself—'In the beginning was the Word, and the Word was with God, and the Word was God'[66]—so, too, God speaks with Himself both at creation and at the Tower of Babel. God said, 'Let Us make man in Our image.'[67] 'Come, let Us go down and there confuse their language.'[68] The singular plurality nature of the Divine is seen at the Creation and at the Tower of Babel when the Persons of the Trinity, including the Christ, speak with one another. God is One yet is an Us. Paradox!"

"Perhaps an even greater paradox is that God is both far[69] and near,"[70] Jonathan pondered as he waded through, in his mind, the deep waters of the nature of God. "Teacher, how do you see this paradox? Do you see Christ in the ancient Scriptures in the midst of this paradox?"

Jesus remained silent for a few moments. Then He stopped. He stood in the middle of the road looking up to the heavens. "Cleopas, has any man ever seen God?"

---

62 John 17:3
63 Genesis 5:24
64 Genesis 6:18-19
65 1 Peter 3:20-21; Hebrews 11:7
66 John 1:1
67 Genesis 1:26
68 Genesis 11:7
69 Job 11:7; Job 36:26
70 Psalm 34:18; Psalm 145:18; Jeremiah 23:23

"No, Teacher. 'No one has seen God at any time.'"[71]

"Then how is it that the Word, Who is God 'dwelt among us and we saw His glory?'"[72]

"Perhaps that paradox is answered by the other paradox? Perhaps the explanation to the seeming contradiction that God can be seen and, yet, never be seen is wrapped up in the paradox of the Trinity."

"Oh, my dear son, Cleopas. You are beginning to see!" Jesus began to walk down the road again.

Catching up with Him, Jonathan pleaded, "Explain this to us, Teacher."

And so, the Teacher taught. "God the Father and God the Holy Spirit have never been seen. God the Son is the member of the Trinity Who is seen by man. This, of course, occurs in its ultimate manifestation in the incarnation.[73] In the ancient Scriptures, Jesus is seen many times in pre-incarnational appearances. He 'appeared to Abram and said, *To your descendants I will give this land.*' Therefore, 'he built an altar there to the LORD who had appeared to him.'[74] Who is the Lord God Who appeared to Abraham if it is true that no man has ever seen God? It is Christ in the Tanakh."

Jesus stopped and looked up into the heavens again. Then He looked down at Himself. "Do you see Him, Cleopas? Do you see Him, Jonathan?"

"We are beginning to see. Help us see more clearly."

Jesus continued. "God appeared to the ninety-nine-year-old Abraham and said to him, '*I am God Almighty; walk before Me, and be blameless. I will establish My covenant between Me and you, and I will multiply you exceedingly.*' Abram fell on his face, and God talked with him, saying, '*As for Me, behold, My covenant is with you, and you will be the father of a multitude of nations. No longer shall your name be called Abram, but your name shall be Abraham; for I will make you the father of a multitude of nations . . . for an everlasting covenant, to be God to you and*

---

71   John 1:18
72   John 1:1, 14, 18
73   Philippians 2:5-8
74   Genesis 12:7

to your descendants after you . . . for an everlasting possession; and I will be their God.'[75] Who is this? He is clearly God. He is also clearly seen by man. He is Jesus in the Tanakh.

"Another pre-incarnational appearance of the Christ—God Who is seen— is in the form of Melchizedek the priest, who is the king of righteousness and the king of peace.[76] Who is this One Who is 'without father, without mother, without genealogy, having neither beginning of days nor end of life, but made like the Son of God, he remains a priest perpetually'?[77] He is none other than Jesus as He is seen in the Tanakh."

Jonathan placed his hand on his chin. He looked to be in deep thought. Suddenly, as if he just remembered something that he could not conjure up for days, he asked, "Teacher, who is 'the angel of the Lord'? Does not the prophet Hosea explain that the angel of the Lord is God Himself?"[78]

"The angel of the Lord often shows up in the Scriptures in pre-incarnate appearances of the Messiah. He appears to Hagar in the wilderness when she is full of fear and hopelessness and blesses her. Hagar responds to this incredible interaction with the angel of the Lord by calling on 'the name of the LORD who spoke to her' and saying, *'You are a God who sees . . . Have I even remained alive here after seeing Him?'*[79] Hagar feels as though she is almost drowning in the quagmire of the paradox of the Trinity. 'God cannot be seen, yet I have seen Him.' She is pulled out of the celestial quicksand by the hand of the Son of God, Who is said to be the angel of the Lord. Later, in an even more desperate situation, Hagar is in the wilderness again when the 'angel of God' interacts with her.[80] God appears in the Scriptures. Yes, Christ appears in the Tanakh."

Jesus stopped walking and pointed to an oak tree on the side of the road. "Let's go sit under the oak for it is like being under the oaks of Mamre."

---

75 Genesis 17:1-5, 7, 8
76 Genesis 14:18-20
77 Hebrews 7:3
78 Hosea 12:3-5
79 Genesis 16:7-13
80 Genesis 21:17-19

"What is the significance of the oaks of Mamre?" asked Cleopas.

"It is at the oaks of Mamre that the Lord appeared to Abraham to tell him that He would end the barrenness of Sarah. God then rhetorically asks, '*Is anything too difficult for the Lord?*'[81] Jesus, when teaching His disciples, says '*with God all things are possible.*'[82] And so, Jesus, before teaching His disciples the same thing—ultimately that God will come to man and be seen by him (as impossible as that may seem)—appears in the ancient Scriptures to Abraham."

"Speaking of Abraham," Jesus said, "Let's consider the mount where God told Abraham to go to sacrifice his son, Isaac. Why would God ask such a thing? It is the same reason why He would ask the same thing of Himself—to sacrifice His own Son on the cross some two thousand years later. Why? Because God so loved the world![83] Abraham, then, was a type of God the Father, and Isaac was a type of God the Son. On that mount, two thousand years before the coming of the Messiah, we see Jesus and the crucifixion event very clearly."

Cleopas looked at Jonathan in bewilderment. "We see the crucifixion of Jesus two thousand years ago?"

"We have already seen Jesus in the ancient Scriptures in many different ways," Jonathan professed. "Who knows? Maybe we will see Him on that mount as well."

Jesus said, "Come off the road. We better sit down for this one. As you will see, there is an uncanny resemblance between the act of sacrificing Isaac and the act of sacrificing Jesus on the cross some two thousand years later. Isaac can be seen as a type—a foreshadowing or example that predicts—of Jesus, and Abraham can be seen as a type of God the Father. Isaac is referred to as Abraham's only son. God said, '*Take now your son, your only son*' and '*I know that you fear God, since you have not withheld your son, your only son, from Me.*'[84]

---

81 Genesis 18:14
82 Matthew 19:26
83 John 3:16
84 Genesis 22:2, 12

Jonathan interjected, "But Isaac was not Abraham's only son."

Jesus continued. "Jesus is God's only Son. Yet it is a very curious proclamation by God to call Isaac the only son of Abraham since, in fact, Abraham has another son in Ishmael. This is another part of the foreshadowing, however, as it matches up Isaac as the only son of the promise with Jesus the ultimate Son of the promise."[85]

"Where is this mount?" asked Cleopas.

Jesus looked to the hills from which they had journeyed. "One of the most incredible aspects of this foreshadowing is seen in the geographical location in which it is taking place. It is on a mount in 'the land of Moriah.'[86] The land of Moriah was in the same place as Golgotha, where Jesus would be crucified nearly two thousand years later.[87] Solomon built the house of the Lord in Jerusalem on Mount Moriah. And so, Abraham and Isaac climb the same hill that the Father and Jesus would climb some two thousand years later."

"That is just incredible!" shouted Jonathan.

"Yes, and the picture gets clearer," assured Jesus. "Even as Jesus entered Jerusalem on a donkey only to become the ultimate sacrificial offering, so, too, Abraham 'saddled his donkey' and split the wood 'for the burnt offering.'[88] A burnt offering is a 'sin offering'[89] that is offered 'to make atonement' or to make payment for sin.[90] This, of course, is what Jesus would become some two thousand years later."[91]

Jonathan, trying to sum things up in his own mind, said, "Jesus Himself, according to the Father's plan, climbs up Mount Moriah to become the payment for sin, even as Isaac two thousand years earlier climbed that very same mount with his father, Abraham, to serve as a burnt offering."

---

85 Hebrews 11:17
86 Genesis 22:2
87 2 Chronicles 3:1
88 Genesis 22:3
89 Leviticus 4:24
90 Leviticus 1:4
91 Hebrews 2:17

"Very good, Jonathan," Jesus encouraged. "But there is much more. For example, prior to the horrific climb up the mount, Jesus went to the Garden of Gethsemane and said to His disciples, 'Sit here.' Similarly, before climbing that very same mount, Abraham said to his young men, 'Stay here.'[92]

"Even the resurrection of Christ is prefigured in the Isaac event. Just before climbing up Mount Moriah, Abraham said to his companions, *'I and the lad will go over there; and we will worship and return to you.'*[93] Abraham knew he was going up the mount to slay his son, yet he said to those who would be waiting for him that both he and Isaac would return. Abraham believed God would raise Isaac from the dead.[94] Indeed, 'On the third day Abraham raised his eyes and saw the place from a distance.'"[95]

Almost ready to weep, Jonathan muttered, "The most haunting picture I have in my mind from the events three days ago is the image of my Lord carrying that cross up the Via Dolorosa, the Way of Suffering, the path He took as He carried His own cross up to Golgotha."[96]

Jesus picked up a large stick and sat back down. "Isaac also carried his own wood up to Golgotha.[97] Before going to the cross, Jesus asked the Father in the Garden of Gethsemane, if He could get out of the upcoming torture, but in the end, He submitted to the Father's will: *'My Father, if it is possible, let this cup pass from Me; yet not as I will, but as You will.'*[98] Isaac, who was a teenager and, thus, capable of, at least, trying to escape from Abraham, spoke to his father in a similar way and, in the end, submitted to his father's will: *'Behold, the fire and the wood, but where is the lamb for the burnt offering? . . . the two of them walked on together.'*"[99]

---

92   Matthew 26:36; Genesis 22:5
93   Genesis 22:5
94   Hebrews 11:17-19
95   Genesis 22:4
96   John 19:17-18
97   Genesis 22:6
98   Matthew 26:39
99   Genesis 22:7-8

Jesus continued, "Jesus is the Lamb of God, who takes away the sin of the world,[100] and Isaac is told that God will provide for Himself the lamb for the burnt offering."[101]

Jesus paused as if emotionally moved Himself. "The next parallel in the stories is the most difficult to understand. You see, after building the altar and binding Isaac to the wood, 'Abraham stretched out his hand and took the knife to slay his son.'"[102]

Cleopas quickly jumped into the conversation. "Well, this is where the comparison stops. Surely, God the Father does not kill God the Son. It was the Roman rulers and the Jewish leaders who did the evil act."

Jesus calmly, almost stoically, explained, "Perplexing as it may be, the prophet Isaiah points ahead to the crucifixion of the Messiah and prophesies, 'the LORD was pleased to crush Him, putting *Him* to grief.'"[103]

Jesus now lifted the tone of His voice and the speed of His speech. "Of course, the hope of mankind rests in the purpose of the crucifixion of Christ. Jesus is the Substitute or Replacement. He dies on the cross in place of man. So, too, the Isaac story includes an incredible substitute: ' . . . a ram caught in the thicket . . . and Abraham . . . offered him up for a burnt offering in the place of his son.'[104] The prophetic response to that interaction was that 'Abraham called the name of that place The LORD Will Provide,' as it is said to this day, 'In the mount of the Lord it will be provided.' Indeed, He will provide 'Himself.'"[105]

"Are you serious?" Cleopas challenged Jesus. "Abraham really said those words two thousand years ago? He really named Golgotha 'The Lord will provide'? And since then, all creation has waited for the Messiah, the Substitute, Who would fulfill the promise, 'In the mount of the Lord it will be provided.'"

---

100 John 1:29
101 Genesis 22:8
102 Genesis 22:10
103 Isaiah 53:10
104 Genesis 22:13
105 Genesis 22:14

"Yes. Yes. Yes," Jonathan cried out as he lifted his hands to Heaven. "Just three days ago I stood there on that hill while Jesus hung on that wood and became my Substitute. In the mount of the Lord, it was provided. He provided Himself. Halleluiah! Halleluiah! Halleluiah!"

Jesus laughed affectionately. "Jonathan, you are not far from the kingdom of God!"

In a monotone voice, Cleopas responded, "I don't even know what to think. All I know is that our Leader was murdered, and I have not seen Him since."

Jesus gently took Cleopas by the face and touched his eyes. "Cleopas, my friend, what a man sees and what a man does not see are truly in the eye of the beholder—unless it is in the beheld. Behold, Cleopas, Abraham saw his Savior. Behold Him!"

Jonathan, still in the joyous waters of his newly found understanding, begged, "Please, Master, share with us the end of the story concerning Abraham and Isaac and how it foreshadows the Gospel message."

"Well, it is not surprising that the story ends with a proclamation of God's grand plan of redemption for all mankind. He proclaims that because of Abraham's obedience He will bless both Abraham, which is Israel, and 'all the nations of the earth.'[106] Similarly, because Jesus obeyed the Father and went to the cross, God's plan of redemption would go forth to 'all the nations.'[107] Just as Jesus said to His disciples, 'Go,'[108] God said to Abraham 'Go.'[109] God's Great Commission began in the book of beginnings. Indeed, Father God, through His only Son Jesus, makes peace between God and man. Incredibly, two thousand years earlier, Father Abraham and his only son Isaac were used as types to foreshadow the coming of this world-changing peace treaty!

---

106 Genesis 22:17-18
107 Matthew 28:19
108 Matthew 28:18
109 Genesis 12:1

"Here, it is prophesied that the Messiah will come from Abraham's seed.[110] Yes, Jesus' genealogy[111] goes through David,[112] through Jesse,[113] through Judah,[114] through Jacob,[115] through Isaac,[116] and all the way back to Abraham. Christ is seen in the Tanakh.

"God has always had the same plan. He calls His people to go to everyone. He calls them to go and be a witness of His love. He tells them that He will be with them always. This is His plan."[117]

With his shoulders slouched and his head down, Cleopas murmured, "I'm not yet sure what I am seeing." Then, suddenly, he rose up, his face pointed straight ahead, and with a renewed sense of energy, he announced, "I may not be sure of what I am seeing but I do know what I would like to see more of. This concept in the Scriptures in which God is seen, even though He cannot be seen, is fascinating to me. These pre-incarnational appearances of the Christ are truly there in the Scriptures. That is amazing!"

"Yes, Cleopas," assured Jesus. "They are seen throughout the Tanakh. When God, for example, reaffirms His covenant with Abraham, He appears to Isaac at Gerar.[118] He appears to Isaac later at Beersheba[119] and affirms the covenant again. Next, He appears to Jacob at Paddan-aram.[120] Later, at Bethel, He not only appears to Jacob, but He wrestles with him."

"God wrestles a man?" Jonathan inquired with somewhat of a sheepish grin on his face.

Jesus continued. "The Man who wrestles with Jacob is identified as God Himself. Jacob saw God face to face.[121] Some twelve hundred years later, the

---

110 Genesis 22:18
111 Luke 3:33-34; Matthew 1:1-3
112 Isaiah 11:1; Psalm 132:11
113 Isaiah 11:10
114 Genesis 49:10
115 Genesis 28:13-14
116 Genesis 26:4
117 Genesis 12:1-3; Genesis 28:14-15; Matthew 28:18-20
118 Genesis 26:1-2
119 Genesis 26:23-24
120 Genesis 31:11-13
121 Genesis 32:24-30

prophet Hosea references that incredible wrestling match and explains that Jacob 'found Him at Bethel and there He spoke with us, even the Lord, the God of hosts, the Lord is His name.'[122] Jesus is seen in the Tanakh."

Still replaying the incredible story in his mind in which Abraham and Isaac walked up that holy mount, Jonathan asked, "Are there others in the Law who can be seen as types of Jesus, those who point to Him?"

"Joseph is a perfect example," answered Jesus. "He is a type of Christ. Christ is seen in Joseph inasmuch as Joseph and his actions clearly point ahead to Christ and His actions. For example, Joseph is greatly loved by his father[123] but is cruelly conspired against and condemned, though innocent, he is sold for silver[124] and thrown into a deep pit by his brothers, who hate him, reject him, and want to kill him,[125] only to be lifted out of the pit[126] to victory and prosperity[127] that is then used to save his brothers, who had tried to put him to death.[128] So, too, the Christ is greatly loved by His Father[129] but is cruelly conspired against and condemned—though innocent–sold for silver,[130] and put into the grave by His own people, who hated Him, rejected Him, and wanted to kill Him,[131] only to be resurrected out of the grave[132] to victory and prosperity[133] that is then used to save His people who had previously killed Him."[134]

Cleopas looked at Jonathan. They both knew what the other was thinking. Almost simultaneously, they exclaimed, "Who is this?"

They just continued to stare at each other, seemingly in confusion, as neither knew exactly Who the other one was, in fact, asking about. Was their

---

122 Hosea 12:3-6
123 Genesis 37:3
124 Genesis 37:28
125 Genesis 37:18
126 Genesis 37:28
127 Genesis 39:1-6; 41:37-45
128 Genesis 45:4-11; Genesis 50:20
129 John 17:26; Matthew 3:17
130 Matthew 26:14-16
131 John 7:1
132 Acts 4:33
133 Hebrews 12:2
134 1 Corinthians 15:57

"Who is this?" question made in reference to the Christ or in reference to this Prophet walking on the road to Emmaus with them? For the first time, they were beginning to wonder if the two were not the same Person. Their hearts were burning within them, but they dared not say to each other what they knew the other was thinking—at least not yet.

"You know, Cleopas," said Jesus, "the Messiah will have disciples from all over the world—those who will follow and obey Him. These disciples are pictured in the Law as it is written, 'The scepter shall not depart from Judah, nor the ruler's staff from between his feet, until Shiloh comes, and to him shall be the obedience of the peoples.'"[135]

Cleopas responded, "The Messiah will have many disciples because He is the Savior."

"Yes," added Jesus. "He is the One Who saves His people. The Messiah is Jesus. Jesus means 'God saves.' This is the very essence of Who Jesus is; He is the Messiah, the Christ, the Savior. He is God. He is God Who saves. Throughout the Tanakh, the salvation of the Savior Who saves is seen repeatedly. Jesus is seen in the Scriptures. 'God saves' is seen in the Torah. 'For Your salvation I wait, O Lord,'[136] and 'The Lord is my strength and song, and He has become my salvation.'[137] 'God saves' is seen in the Prophets. 'I, even I, am the Lord, and there is no Savior besides Me,'[138] and 'Salvation is from the Lord.'[139] 'God saves' is seen in the Writings. 'Wondrously show Your lovingkindness Savior of those who take refuge at Your right hand,'[140] and 'Save us, O God of our salvation.'[141] Jesus—'God saves'—is seen in the Scriptures."

---

135 Genesis 49:10
136 Genesis 49:18
137 Exodus 15:2
138 Isaiah 43:11
139 Jonah 2:9
140 Psalm 17:7
141 1 Chronicles 16:35

CHAPTER 2

CONVERSING IN EXODUS

Jonathan was definitely one who contemplated things. He would go over and over in his mind the profound mysteries that were being explained. Spontaneously, he would then blurt out a question. "Who else is like Joseph? Who else is a clear type of Christ?"

"Let us look at Moses," Jesus offered. "Moses, by the mighty sovereign hand of God, was protected from the wicked plan of Pharaoh who wanted to massacre newborn Jewish males.[1] He was kept safe as an infant in Egypt[2] and then later taken out of Egypt in the Exodus[3] and used as a mighty vessel of the Lord who walked before God and men in great humility[4] even as the people persistently grumbled against Him.[5] Moses, thus, stands as a type of Christ who, by the mighty sovereign hand of God, was protected from the wicked plan of Herod who wanted to massacre newborn Jewish males.[6] He was kept safe as an infant in Egypt[7] and then called out of Egypt[8] as the prophet Hosea said, 'When Israel *was* a youth I loved him, and out of Egypt I called My son.'[9] He was used as a mighty vessel of the Lord who walked before God and men

---

1   Exodus 1:16, 22
2   Exodus 2:3-10
3   Exodus 12:31-33; Exodus 12:40-42
4   Numbers 12:3
5   Numbers 14:2, 27, 36
6   Matthew 2:16
7   Matthew 2:13-14
8   Matthew 2:15
9   Hosea 11:1

in great humility[10] even as the people consistently grumbled against Him.[11] Moses, as a type of Christ, reflected Him and His actions in such a way as to point to Him even some fifteen hundred years before Him."

Jesus put his arm around Cleopas as they continued to walk. "Cleopas, how is it that God has never been seen, yet He is seen?"

"He is seen as the Son of God, the Christ."[12]

Jonathan wanted to be a part of this conversation. "As you have shown us, Teacher, the Divine, pre-incarnate appearances as the angel of the Lord are established in the Scriptures when the prophet Hosea explains that the angel of the Lord is God Himself."[13]

Jesus again began to teach. "The angel of the Lord appeared to Moses in the burning bush[14] and revealed Himself as Savior.[15] After Moses failed to fulfill the covenant and disobeyed with respect to circumcision,[16] He again appeared to him as Judge.[17] At the burning bush, the pre-incarnate Christ made known to Moses His name, I AM.[18] That name is His in perpetuity; thus, He referred to Himself that way fifteen hundred years later during the days of His ministry."[19]

Off on the side of the road was a shepherd who was tending his sheep. Staring at the shepherd, Jesus inquired, "Jonathan, what is your work?"

"I am a tentmaker."

"Do you know that Jesus took the work of His disciples and turned it into the work of God?"

"Yes. He told those fishermen that He would make them fishers of men."[20]

---

10 Philippians 2:3-8
11 Luke 15:2; 19:7; John 6:43
12 John 1:1, 14-18
13 Hosea 12:3-5
14 Exodus 3:2
15 Exodus 3:7-9
16 Exodus 4:25-26
17 Exodus 4:24
18 Exodus 3:14
19 John 8:58
20 Matthew 4:19

"Correct! Similarly, God told Moses and Aaron the same thing. He used their work—that of a shepherd—and turned it into God's work. He took the very tool of their work, the staff, and used it instead for His miraculous works.[21] In this way, Jesus' employment of His disciples to do His work is prefigured by God's use of Moses to do His work."

"What else about Moses points to Christ?" asked Cleopas.

"Moses stands as a type of the Christ in terms of their ministries. Like the Christ,[22] Moses was rejected by the rulers of the world[23] and by his own people.[24] Moses even questioned his sense of being separated from God[25] just as the Son of God, paradoxically, questioned being separated from the Father.[26] Jesus took the sin of the world upon Himself and, in so doing, experienced spiritual death; in an unexplainable way, He was separated from Himself. This may be impossible to understand but it does show the price that had to be paid by God for the redemption of man.[27] One final comparison is that Moses was reassured of the efficacy of his ministry.[28] So, too, the Christ is reassured of the success of His ministry.[29]

"Come, my friends," directed Jesus. "There is a well just down that hill. Let us go and refresh ourselves."

As the men left the road and began to walk down the hill, Jesus took the time to reestablish His original point. "The New Covenant that has now come in Christ is the continuation and completion of the Old Covenant. Ultimately, Christ is the continuation and completion of 'God saw all that He had made, and behold, it was very good.'[30] He is the correction and rerouting of that which is not good, back to that which is good. This is, of course, redemption.

---

21   Exodus 4:2; 7:12; 14:16; 8:16; 9:23; 10:13
22   Luke 17:25; Mark 8:31
23   Exodus 5:2
24   Exodus 5:20-21
25   Exodus 5:22-23
26   Matthew 27:46
27   2 Corinthians 5:21; John 1:29; Romans 6:23
28   Exodus 7:1-5
29   Hebrews 2:10-18
30   Genesis 1:31

It is to deem something one way—it was very good—then to deem it another way—it is very bad—and then to redeem it in its original way—it is very good. His Story is moving from the tree of life in the garden[31] to the tree of the knowledge of good and evil[32] in that same garden, and then back to the original tree of life in the perfected garden yet to come.[33] This is redemption, and Jesus is the purchaser of redemption."

"So, then, Jesus is seen in His redemptive work in the Scriptures," Jonathan decisively declared.

"Yes, Jonathan. Remember My words when I began to walk with you on this road to Emmaus—that all things which are written about the Christ 'in the Law of Moses and the Prophets and the Psalms must be fulfilled.'[34] Christ is continually seen in the Tanakh."

The three men sat down at the well. Cleopas, responding to what Jesus had just said, contributed, "When I think of redemption and salvation in the Scriptures, I think of the Exodus."

Jesus took a drink. "In an astonishing way, the Exodus is analogous to the final events of the life of Christ. In the Passover, prior to the Exodus of the Jews from Egypt, Jesus' death on the cross at Calvary was foreshadowed.[35] Jesus, the Son of God, is the Lamb of God who takes away the sin of the world.[36] This fulfills the use of the blood from an unblemished lamb to pass over the sin of the people.[37] The Passover lamb[38] prefigures the Son of God, the sacrificial Lamb, Who enters the world fifteen hundred years later. Even the spreading of the blood of the Passover lamb on the doorposts and on the lintel created a sort of cross of dripping blood.[39] It is the substitutionary

---

31   Genesis 2:9
32   Genesis 2:16-17
33   Revelation 2:7
34   Luke 24:44
35   1 Corinthians 5:7
36   John 1:29, 34
37   Exodus 12:5, 13
38   Exodus 12:21
39   Exodus 12:7

blood that serves as a propitiation that God must see in order for sin not to be seen. 'For the Lord will pass through to smite the Egyptians; and when He sees the blood on the lintel and on the two doorposts, the Lord will pass over the door and will not allow the destroyer to come in to your houses to smite you.'[40] This substitutionary blood, ultimately, is the blood of the Christ."[41]

Jesus took another drink. "The Passover, followed by the parting of the Red Sea in the Exodus,[42] anticipates the resurrection of Jesus Christ while the Law given at Sinai[43] portends the Spirit who will be given on the day of Pentecost. Incredibly, both progressions of events—the resurrection until the giving of the Spirit on the day of Pentecost and the leaving of Egypt until the giving of the Law at Sinai—occur over a period of fifty days. With respect to the Exodus, the Passover happens on the fourteenth day of the first month.[44] Over the next two days, the Israelites made their way out of Egypt, what one might call a resurrection from their bondage and what was most significantly symbolized by the parting of the Red Sea. This day, the first days after the Passover and the 'day' of being resurrected out of the bondage of Egypt, would come to be called the Day of First Fruits. The giving of the Law to Moses on Mount Sinai happens sometime soon after the first day of the third month. That's a total of fifty days. This would come to be called the Feast of Pentecost that would occur after the Feast of Weeks. And, yes, you might guess this. Jesus, the Passover Lamb, was resurrected on the Day of First Fruits, and the Spirit will be poured out after the Feast of Weeks on the day of Pentecost—exactly fifty days!"

"Does Jesus actually show up in the Exodus?" asked Cleopas.

"Once again He shows up as 'the angel of God.' He went before the people in a pillar of cloud by day and a pillar of fire by night to lead them

---

40   Exodus 12:23
41   Romans 3:21-26
42   Exodus 14
43   Exodus 19-20
44   Exodus 12:6; Exodus 19:1; Luke 22:15; Leviticus 23:6-14; 1 Corinthians 5:6-8; 1 Corinthians 15:20-23; Leviticus 23:9-14; Matthew 28:1-6; Leviticus 23:15-21; Deuteronomy 16:9-12; Acts 2:1-4; Acts 1:3-5

out of Egypt.[45] The Messiah saves the people, and then He guides them as His presence continues His saving action. Christ is seen in the Tanakh."

Jesus continued. "The Son of God is the Redeemer. He is the Savior. He is the One Who guides and Whose presence is very real. He is also the Provider. In fact, if you care to believe it, He is the Manna that God rained down from Heaven to feed the Israelites in the wilderness.[46] The Christ is the Bread of Life[47] Who is seen as the Provider in all the Scriptures."[48] And so, when the Israelites were thirsty in the wilderness, He became the Rock from which spiritual water came that the people could drink.[49] Ultimately, the water that comes from Christ, the Rock, is the water of eternal life.[50]

"Remember, Cleopas and Jonathan," Jesus instructed, "you cannot see God, but you *can* see God. You can see God because you can see Christ. The Son of God is in the Father and the Father is in the Son, for they are one God.[51] When you see the Son, you have seen the Father, for the Son is the exact Representation of the Father.[52] The Son is the 'Angel' Who led the Israelites in the wilderness and Who was to be obeyed since the Father's name was in Him.[53] The Christ is seen in the Tanakh."

Still sitting at the well, Jesus passed His cup to Cleopas. "Christ's blood that is shed for the forgiveness of sins[54] is pictured throughout the Scriptures. It is His blood that saves men from their sins.[55] Moses exhibits this when he 'took the blood and sprinkled it on the people.'[56] This blood is a shadow of the blood to come. In either case, however, forgiveness must be accompanied

---

45   Exodus 14:19; Exodus 13:21-22
46   Exodus 16:4
47   John 6:31-40
48   Philippians 1:19-20
49   1 Corinthians 10:4
50   John 4:10-14
51   John 14:8-11
52   Hebrews 1:3
53   Exodus 23:20-23
54   Mark 14:24
55   Hebrews 13:8
56   Exodus 24:8

by the shedding of blood.[57] And so, the Christ is seen in the New Covenant in the context of the presentation of the blood of the covenant.[58] He is seen in the Old Covenant in a pre-incarnate appearance in the context of Moses' presentation of the blood of the covenant as 'they saw the God of Israel; and under His feet there appeared to be a pavement of sapphire, as clear as the sky itself. Yet He did not stretch out His hand against the nobles of the sons of Israel; and they saw God, and they ate and drank.'"[59]

Cleopas stood up. "We should begin our journey again." Jonathan put out his hand, and Cleopas pulled him up from where he was sitting by the well. Jesus rose up and put His arms around both men, and they began to walk up the hill together.

Back on the road to Emmaus, Jesus suggested, "Let's talk about the tabernacle. The tabernacle of the Old Covenant[60] is analogous to the redemptive work of Jesus.[61] The tabernacle represents the Old Covenant's physical manifestation of the New Covenant's spiritual reality concerning the work of Christ. Each of the seven stations of the tabernacle has its fulfillment in Jesus."

"And so, Jesus is seen seven times in the tabernacle?" Cleopas probed.

"Let's look together. The first station of the tabernacle was the brazen altar that was used for animal sacrifices and signified repentance and payment for sins. This station of the tabernacle had its fulfillment in the blood of Jesus Christ. The second station of the tabernacle, the Laver, was used for cleansing and washing. The people could not go beyond this point in the tabernacle. It represented the need of, and provision for, cleansing. It is the cross that is the fulfillment of this station of the tabernacle. Without Jesus' cleansing of you through His death on the cross, you would have no part with God. When

---

57   Hebrews 9:22
58   Matthew 26:28
59   Exodus 24:10-11
60   Exodus 25-30
61   Hebrews 9-10

Peter said to Him, 'Never shall You wash my feet!,' Jesus answered him, 'If I do not wash you, you have no part with Me.'"[62]

"I never thought of the tabernacle in this way," Jonathan contemplated. "What else might we learn, Teacher?"

Jesus continued, "The third station of the tabernacle was the Table of Showbread that was the representation of God's presence and provision and signified trust in God. Of course, Jesus is your Provision; your trust must be in Him, and He is the Bread of Life.[63]

"The fourth station, the Altar of Incense, was used for intercession for the people signifying prayer and forgiveness. Jesus is a Sweet Smell of incense and intercession.[64] The fifth station, the Golden Lampstand, represented God the Light signifying ministry and missions. This is fulfilled in Jesus, the Light of the world.[65] The sixth station, the veil, represented the separation between God and man. You know, it was torn when Jesus died on the cross three days ago. It now signifies the fact that relationship with God is made possible by the slaying of Jesus' flesh on the cross.[66] The seventh station, the Ark of the Covenant, represented the presence of God. The priest could only enter it once each year. Now, in Christ, you can enjoy the presence of God continually since Christ is in you."[67] Christ is seen in the tabernacle!"

They passed a group of men who were going the other direction on the road. Jesus asked them as they passed by, "Who do people say that the Christ is?"

"He is the Savior," answered one of them.

Another yelled out, "He is the Redeemer."

A third added, "He is the Provider."

---

62 John 13:8
63 John 6:48
64 Revelation 8:4
65 John 8:12
66 Hebrews 10:19-20
67 Colossians 1:27

Both groups of men continued walking in their own directions. Jesus now turned to His companions and asked, "Who do you say the Christ is?"

"He is Jesus," Cleopas said matter-of-factly.

"He is God," Jonathan said more emphatically.

"Yes, my friends," Jesus replied. "Jesus Christ is God. And so, God says to Moses, 'You cannot see My face, for no man can see Me and live!'[68] Yet, 'the Lord used to speak to Moses face to face, just as a man speaks to his friend.'[69] God cannot be seen, yet He is seen. This is the Christ. He is the Person of the Trinity who can be seen while the other Persons cannot be seen. Christ is the exact representation of the nature of God both in the New and Old Covenants.[70] Christ is how God is seen both in the New and in the Old. Christ is seen over and over again and in a variety of ways in the Tanakh."

---

68 Exodus 33:20
69 Exodus 33:11
70 Hebrews 1:3

CHAPTER 3

CONVERSING IN LEVITICUS, NUMBERS, DEUTERONOMY

Up ahead, a shepherd was leading his flock from one side of the road to the other. Jesus looked at Cleopas and asked, "Why is the Messiah called the Lamb of God?"

"Because He becomes a Sacrifice."

"In the New Covenant, the Christ becomes the fulfillment of the sacrificial system[1] that was instituted under the Old Covenant with its various offerings.[2] The burnt offering[3] typifies Christ's total offering that provides a propitiation for general sin.[4] It demonstrates His complete surrender to the Father's will.[5] The meal offering[6] represents Christ's sinless service.[7] The peace offering[8] points to the fellowship with God that can be had by man because of the work of the cross.[9] The sin offering[10] typifies Christ as the One Who bears the guilt of sinners.[11] The guilt offering[12] demonstrates Christ's payment for the

---

1   Ephesians 5:2
2   Leviticus 1-7
3   Leviticus 1
4   1 John 2:1-2
5   Luke 22:42
6   Leviticus 2
7   1 Peter 1:18-19; 2 Corinthians 5:21
8   Leviticus 3
9   Matthew 27:50-51
10   Leviticus 4
11   1 John 1:7-9; 2 Corinthians 5:21
12   Leviticus 5

destruction of sin. Indeed, on the cross, Christ said, 'It is finished'; 'It is paid in full.'[13] The Messiah is seen in the sacrificial system."

"What about the priests who administered those sacrifices?" Jonathan asked.

"Jesus is seen in the Old Covenant's priesthood. Made up of Aaron and his descendants,[14] that priesthood was fulfilled once and for all in Christ, the High Priest. 'For it was fitting . . . to have such a high priest, holy, innocent, undefiled, separated from sinners and exalted above the heavens; who does not need daily, like those high priests, to offer up sacrifices, first for His own sins and then for the *sins* of the people, because this He did once for all when He offered up Himself. For the Law appoints men as high priests who are weak, but the word of the oath, which came after the Law, *appoints* a Son, made perfect forever.'[15] Jesus is seen in the Tanakh."

"So, the atoning blood—whether it is that of the Old Covenant or that of the New Covenant—is that which provides for the forgiveness of sins?" inquired Cleopas.

"Yes. Jesus provides the atoning blood. Even as Christ said, 'This is My blood of the covenant, which is poured out for many for forgiveness of sins,'[16] so, too, is it stated in the Law, 'For the life of the flesh is in the blood, and I have given it to you on the altar to make atonement for your souls; for it is the blood by reason of the life that makes atonement.'[17] Indeed, the salvation provided by Christ is seen in the Scriptures.

"Christ is also seen in the feasts of the Old Covenant as He becomes their fulfillment in the New Covenant.[18] The Feast of the Passover[19] typifies the Lamb of God and His substitutionary death.[20] Christ died on the Passover.[21] The

---

13   John 19:30
14   Leviticus 8
15   Hebrews 7:26-28
16   Matthew 26:28
17   Leviticus 17:11
18   1 Corinthians 5:7-8; Leviticus 23
19   Leviticus 23:5
20   1 Corinthians 5:7; John 1:29
21   Luke 22:15

Feast of Unleavened Bread[22] points to the sanctification of those who believe in Christ.[23] The Feast of First Fruits[24] represents Jesus' resurrection, as He is the First Fruits of all who will be raised from the dead.[25] Christ rose on the day of First Fruits, the day after the Sabbath.[26] The Feast of Weeks[27] will be fulfilled at Pentecost—fifty days after the day of First Fruits—when the Spirit will be poured out after Christ's ascension.[28] The Feast of Trumpets[29] will be fulfilled when Christ returns at the sound of a trumpet that will call His people to Himself.[30] The Feast of the Day of Atonement[31] is fulfilled in Christ, Who atones for sins once and for all.[32] The Feast of Tabernacles[33] typifies the promise of the outpouring of the Holy Spirit after Jesus' ascension[34] and, ultimately, as the prophet Joel writes, it typifies the work of the Holy Spirit that leads to the second coming of Christ.[35] Jesus is certainly seen in the feasts."

Cleopas stepped ahead quickly and then stopped and turned to face his companions. He held Jonathan's arm on his one side and Jesus' arm on his other side and then maneuvered in such a way as to have the three of them form a sort of circle. "What about seeing all three Persons of God at the same time in the Scriptures?"

"Of course," Jesus responded. "Take, for example, the account of the people complaining as they wandered in the wilderness. All three Persons of the Trinity were clearly involved there. First, you see the Son of God, the One Who goes down to men.[36] He takes the Holy Spirit from Moses and

---

22   Leviticus 23:6-8
23   1 Corinthians 5:6-8
24   Leviticus 23:9-14
25   1 Corinthians 15:20-23
26   Matthew 28:1-6
27   Leviticus 23:15-21; Deuteronomy 16:9-12
28   Acts 2:1-4: Acts 1:3-5
29   Leviticus 23:23-25
30   1 Corinthians 15:51-52; 1 Thessalonians 4:16-17
31   Leviticus 23:26-32
32   Romans 3:24-26; Hebrews 9:7
33   Leviticus 23:33-43
34   John 7:2, 37
35   Joel 2:28-31
36   Numbers 11:17, 25; John 6:42

places Him upon the seventy elders who then begin to prophesy.[37] Then you see the Father, the One Who judges men, strike the people with sickness because of their greed.[38] So, the Christ is seen together with the Father and the Holy Spirit in the Tanakh.

"Jesus is the Person of the Godhead that is seen by men. He is seen in the Tanakh, most definitively, in a variety of pre-incarnate appearances. In one of those appearances, Moses sees His very form as Christ speaks of him, saying, 'With him I speak mouth to mouth, even openly, and not in dark sayings, and he beholds the form of the LORD.'[39] Jesus is repeatedly seen in the Tanakh in these amazing ways."

An odd sounding gulp suddenly came from Jonathan as though he had just figured something out. "What about the unblemished red heifer sacrifice that is slaughtered outside the camp?[40] That certainly must be a way in which the Christ is seen in the Law."

"Indeed, Jonathan," Jesus said in a sort of congratulatory tone. "It points to Messiah's crucifixion. It foreshadows His death[41] and burial.[42] As you rightly said, Jonathan, the red heifer sacrifice certainly is a way in which the Christ is seen in the Law."

Jesus walked closer to Cleopas. He put His hand on His shoulder and spoke softly. "How about you, Cleopas? What do you see?"

Cleopas had already been thinking about an answer to such a question. He paused. "Well, the first thing that I think of is the fiery serpent that Moses was told to lift up on a standard."

Almost looking like he was about to cry, Cleopas paused, looked down at the ground, and cleared his throat. "That serpent on the standard looks a lot like Jesus on the cross that I saw three days ago."

---

37 Numbers 11:24-29
38 Numbers 11:33-34
39 Numbers 12:8
40 Numbers 19:2-3
41 Numbers 19:3
42 Numbers 19:9

"So it does," agreed Jesus. "While the people were seemingly stuck in the wilderness, they began to complain against Moses and God.[43] God sent fiery serpents to bite the people, and many of them died.[44] These snakes represent sin and its wages.[45] The people repent, and God tells Moses, '*Make a fiery serpent, and set it on a standard; and it shall come about, that everyone who is bitten, when he looks at it, he will live.*'[46] And so, Moses made a bronze serpent and put it on the standard and whoever looked at it lived. That is to say, sin is put on Jesus on the cross and whoever believes in Him shall be saved. 'As Moses lifted up the serpent in the wilderness, even so must the Son of Man be lifted up' and take upon Himself the sin of man in order to pay the price for that sin 'so that whoever believes will in Him have eternal life.'"[47]

Jesus looked deep into the eyes of Cleopas. "Yes, Cleopas, you will cry. You will cry tears of joy, for Jesus is seen in the Scriptures as He Who will bring you life."

"It is incredible, and certainly ironic, that Jesus is seen in the Scriptures in the displaying of a snake," mused Jonathan.

"How much more incredible is it for Jesus to show up in the midst of a talking donkey?" Jesus added and then He explained, "The prophet Balaam was traveling on a donkey en route to perform a service at the request of Balak the king of Moab. A pre-incarnate appearance of the Son of God—the Angel of the Lord,[48] as He is so often referred to in the Scriptures—was seen by Balaam's donkey, and yet, Balaam denied the actuality of the appearance, striking his donkey three times. Each time the donkey responded with rhetorical questions addressed to Balaam. 'Then the Lord opened the eyes of Balaam, and he saw the angel of the Lord standing in the way with his drawn sword in his hand; and he bowed all the way to the ground. Then the angel of

---

43 Numbers 21:4-5
44 Numbers 21:6
45 Romans 6:23
46 Numbers 21:7-8
47 John 3:14-15; 2 Corinthians 5:21; John 19:30
48 Numbers 22:22-35

the Lord said to him, "Why have you struck your donkey these three times? Behold, I have come out as an adversary, because your way was contrary to me."[49] Balaam, in this instance, stood as a type of Peter, who denied Christ three times.[50] Interestingly, like Peter who was restored three times,[51] so, too, Balaam, through his prophesies, was restored three times."[52]

"So, the angel of the Lord in that scene is God?" Cleopas probed.

"Yes. He is referenced as God,[53] the Lord,[54] and the Almighty.[55] Christ is seen in the Tanakh.

"There is more from Balaam," Jesus continued. "He actually saw the birth of the Messiah. 'I see him, but not now; I behold him, but not near; a star shall come forth from Jacob, a scepter shall rise from Israel.'[56] At Messiah's birth the star appeared, and the magi followed it to find the Ruler Who would come from Judah by way of Jacob.[57] Balaam sees the Messiah in the Tanakh."

Just then, they passed by a merchant who was selling pieces of fish. "Let us sit by the side of the road and have something to eat," offered Jonathan. "I will buy some pieces of fish and a loaf of bread, and we can take a break from our journey and strengthen ourselves."

While Jonathan was bargaining with the merchant, Jesus and Cleopas found a place to sit down in the shade. Jonathan rejoined his companions and passed around the food.

"Thank you for feeding us, Jonathan," Jesus said with a smile.

"Oh, but it is my great honor, Teacher, as you have been feeding us these past hours while we have been walking on the road. There is such an abundance of different ways in which the Christ is seen in the Law."

---

49   Numbers 22:31-32
50   Matthew 26:75
51   John 21:15-17
52   Numbers 24:10
53   Numbers 23:4
54   Numbers 23:16
55   Numbers 24:4
56   Numbers 24:17
57   Matthew 2:1-11

Jesus took from the bread. "There is another way we can see Christ in the Law. The sinner takes his refuge in Christ. Without Him, judgment would be unavoidable. So, too, it is with the manslayer and the six cities of refuge. The manslayer must flee to the city of refuge, or judgment will be unavoidable.[58] This city is Christ. Yes, Jonathan, Christ is seen in the Law."

The three continued to eat. "Cleopas, I have a question for you," asserted Jesus. "What is the most often-recited Scripture?"

Cleopas thought for a few moments. "It would most certainly be the Shema."

"Ah, yes," Jesus agreed.

Jonathan began to recite the holy declaration. "'Hear O Israel! The Lord is our God, the Lord is one!'"[59]

Jesus began to teach. "The Lord your God is One. More specifically, He is an Echad, a diverse Unity,[60] as opposed to a yachid, a non-diverse unity.[61] God is One—a compound unity. He is God the Father, God the Son, and God the Holy Spirit. He is One God in three distinct Persons. In this way, the Shema refers to the Trinity and, thus, to Christ."

As the men began to finish their lunch, Cleopas humbly said to Jesus, "Teacher, now I have a question for You."

"Ask it, my friend."

"Who is it in the Law that stands as the one who reflects Christ the most?"

"The one who most definitively stands as a type of Christ is Moses.[62] Moses said to the people, '*The LORD your God will raise up for you a prophet like me from among you, from your countrymen, you shall listen to him.*'[63] Indeed, both Moses and Christ are prophets, priests, kings, kinsman redeemers,[64] deliverers, lawgivers, and mediators. Both are endangered in infancy and are hidden for

---

58 Numbers 35:6
59 Deuteronomy 6:4
60 Numbers 13:23; Genesis 1:5; Genesis 2:24
61 Judges 11:34
62 Acts 3:20-23
63 Deuteronomy 18:15
64 Exodus 6:6; Luke 1:68

a time in Egypt.[65] Both voluntarily renounce the power and wealth they could have had in order to be used by God to deliver the people.[66]

"Most certainly, Cleopas," Jesus concluded, "Moses is a type of Christ, who reflects Him in the Law.

"Sometimes, it is Moses' instructions from God to the people that point to the Messiah. 'If a man has committed a sin worthy of death and he is put to death, and you hang him on a tree, his corpse shall not hang all night on the tree, but you shall surely bury him on the same day (for he who is hanged is accursed of God).'[67] Three days ago you saw the crucifixion of the Messiah as He hung on a tree[68] as One Who is accursed 'having become a curse for us.'"[69]

"And so, you see, Cleopas and Jonathan, how the Messiah is seen in the Law numerous times and in various ways. Yes, the Law[70] reveals the Christ!"

---

65 Exodus 2:1-3; Matthew 2:13-15
66 Hebrews 11:24-26; Philippians 2:5-7
67 Deuteronomy 21:22-23
68 Galatians 3:13
69 2 Corinthians 5:21
70 Genesis; Exodus; Leviticus; Numbers; Deuteronomy

NEVI'IM
CONVERSATIONS
(THE PROPHETS)

CHAPTER 4

CONVERSING IN JOSHUA, JUDGES

"We are still several hours from our destination," Cleopas calculated. He stood and began to walk toward the road. Jonathan and Jesus followed him.

Back on the road to Emmaus, the conversations began again. This time, the conversations focused on the Prophets.

"You know, Cleopas," Jesus proposed, "as much as the Christ is seen in the Law, He is seen just as much in the Prophets."

"Show us, Teacher," Jonathan begged. "We want to see Him!"

"Even as Moses in the Law is a type of Christ, so, too, Joshua in the Prophets is a type of Christ to come. Joshua is the Hebrew equivalent of Jesus. Even as Jesus supersedes the Mosaic law[1] and wins the victory not able to be had by the Law—'For the Law was given through Moses; grace and truth were realized through Jesus Christ'[2]—so, too, Joshua secedes Moses and wins the victory not able to be had by Him.[3] It is through Jesus that they 'overwhelmingly conquer'[4] and that God the Father leads 'many sons to glory'[5] and to victory.[6] Joshua prefigures Jesus in that he successfully leads his people into their possessions.[7] In all of this, Joshua—which means 'God saves'—is

---

1   Romans 8:2-4
2   John 1:17
3   Joshua 1:1-3
4   Romans 8:37
5   Hebrews 2:10
6   2 Corinthians 2:14
7   Joshua 1:4-9; 11:23

a type of Jesus, which also means 'God saves.' Jesus is seen in the Scriptures through Joshua as Joshua points to the greater One to come."

"As you have taught us, Teacher," Jonathan affirmed, "it is the blood of Christ that saves."

"You are a good student, Jonathan," Jesus acknowledged as He put His hand on Jonathan's shoulder.

Jonathan smiled.

Jesus used the opportunity to explain yet another "Christ sighting" in the Prophets. "Even as the blood on the doorposts in Egypt served as a signal for the judgment of God to pass over the Israelites assuring their protection,[8] so, too, the cord of scarlet thread in Rahab's window served as a marker for protection. In each case, these signs pointed to the blood on the cross of Christ that would even more completely assure the deliverance and protection of those who trusted in it.[9] Incredibly, the Gentile woman, Rahab, gets grafted into the genealogy of Christ[10] and is used to point to Him."

Cleopas felt like it was time for him to contribute to the conversation. "I feel like I don't know what to say," muttered Cleopas. "All I keep thinking is, Jesus keeps showing up in the Scriptures. Maybe He will show up here on the road to Emmaus."

Jesus laughed.

"Maybe He will, Cleopas. Maybe He will." Jesus then added, "He certainly showed up when He appeared to Joshua in a startling pre-incarnate appearance. Joshua reports that 'he lifted up his eyes and looked, and behold, a man was standing opposite him with his sword drawn in his hand.' Joshua said to him, *Are you for us or for our adversaries?* He said, *No; rather I indeed come now as captain of the host of the LORD.* Joshua fell on his face, and bowed down, and said to him, *What has my lord to say to his servant?* The captain of the LORD's host said to him, *Remove your sandals*

---

8   Exodus 12:7, 23
9   Romans 3:21-26; Hebrews 9:19-22
10   Matthew 1:5

from your feet, for the place where you are standing is holy. And Joshua did so.'[11] Who was this 'captain of the Lord's host' Who Joshua worshipped and Who commanded him to remove his sandals because the ground on which He was standing was holy? It is the same God Who appeared to Moses in a burning bush and Who said, 'Remove your sandals from your feet for the place on which you are standing is holy ground.'[12] Christ appears in the Tanakh.

"In another appearance of the Lord as the 'Angel of the Lord,' the people of Israel respond with repentance and worship[13] toward this One Who speaks in first person as He proclaims His Divine activities. He came to Bochim and he said, *'I brought you up out of Egypt and led you into the land which I have sworn to your fathers; and I said, I will never break My covenant with you, and as for you, you shall make no covenant with the inhabitants of this land; you shall tear down their altars. But you have not obeyed Me; what is this you have done? Therefore I also said, I will not drive them out before you; but they will become as thorns in your sides and their gods will be a snare to you.'*[14] It is the Son of God, Who is seen by men, Who speaks as God when He appears and speaks to the people."

Cleopas, seeming to suddenly focus back in on the conversation, abruptly declared, "Teacher, in the former Prophets, we see the judges. Do these judges point to the Christ?"

"Indeed, they do," confirmed Jesus. "They stand as a type of Christ, even as they serve as deliverers of the people from their oppressors and Christ serves as the ultimate Deliverer of all people from their sin.[15] Even as a judge is a savior and a ruler, so, too, Christ is the Savior and the King. Some judges were prophets, like Samuel; others were priests, like Eli; and still others were rulers, like Gideon. Thus, the cumulative identity of the judges portrays the

---

11   Joshua 5:13-15
12   Exodus 3:1-6
13   Judges 2:5
14   Judges 2:1-4
15   Romans 8:1-2

cumulative ministry of Christ: Prophet,[16] Priest,[17] and King.[18] In this way, Jesus is certainly seen in the Prophets."

Again, Cleopas seemed to be somewhere else as Jesus concluded His teaching concerning the judges.

"Cleopas!" Jesus whispered as He gently put His arm around him and shook him tenderly. "Where are you?"

Cleopas perked up like a student in a classroom who had just been called upon after having wandered off in thought for a few moments. "I am here, Teacher. I have been pondering the depths of a perplexing question. How can a man see God and live?"

Jesus paused as He looked up into the heavens. "Indeed, no man can see God and live, but he shall surely die.[19] Thus, Gideon feared for his life when he saw the 'Angel of the Lord,' Whom he understood to be God.[20] Yet, God assured him, saying, 'Peace to you, do not fear; you shall not die.'"[21]

Cleopas seemed a bit frustrated. "How can it be that he shall both surely die and surely not die?"

"This paradox is rooted in another paradox that is not really another, but the same—that is, the paradox of the Trinity. How can it be that God is both seen and not seen?[22] God the Father is not seen, yet God the Son is seen. Appearances of the 'Angel of the Lord' in the Scriptures are pre-incarnate appearances of the Son of God. Christ is seen in the Scriptures."

Jonathan was tossing a stone back and forth from hand to hand. "Teacher, you have shown us how Christ has appeared in the Scriptures repeatedly as the 'Angel of the Lord' or the 'Angel of God.' The incarnate One Whom we beheld for these past years existed before Abraham[23]; He

---

16 Acts 3:22
17 Hebrews 3:1
18 Matthew 2:2
19 Exodus 33:20; Genesis 32:30
20 Judges 6:11-24
21 Judges 6:23
22 John 1:1, 14, 18
23 John 8:58

existed before time.[24] In this way, His pre-incarnate appearances are able to be understood."

Jesus thought for a moment. "Yes, let me add another instance in which the pre-incarnate Christ appears. He appeared to the wife of Manoah,[25] who was barren but would eventually give birth to the judge, Samson.[26] This 'Angel of God'[27] referred to Himself as the Lord; and Manoah and his wife, therefore, offered sacrifices to Him and worshipped Him.[28] The 'Angel of the Lord' then performed wonders.[29] Beyond this, He described Himself as One Whose name is incomprehensible.[30] Who was this Angel of God, this Angel of the Lord? It was God Himself. When referring to the Angel of the Lord, Manoah said to his wife, '*We shall surely die, for we have seen God.*'[31] Nevertheless, they did not die since they did not see the God Who cannot be seen, God the Father, but did see the God Who can be seen, God the Son.[32] The Son of God often appears in the ancient Scriptures."

Jesus continued to speak about Samson. "Samson is most certainly a type of Christ as his life points to Him in numerous ways. In the case of both Samson and Christ, an angel foretold their birth.[33] Both men are separated unto God as Nazarenes.[34] Both acted in the power of the Holy Spirit.[35] Both were victorious over their enemies.[36] Both were rejected and mocked.[37] Both, by their death, saw their ultimate victory over their enemies.[38] Herein, Christ is seen in the former Prophets once again."

---

24   Colossians 1:17
25   Judges 13:2-3
26   Judges 13:24
27   Judges 13:9
28   Judges 13:16, 19-20
29   Judges 13:19
30   Judges 13:18
31   Judges 13:21-22
32   John 1:1, 14, 18
33   Judges 13:3-5; Luke 1:30-31
34   Judges 13:5; Matthew 2:23
35   Judges 13:25; 14:6; 15:14; Luke 3:22; 4:1, 14, 18
36   Judges 15:15; Hebrews 2:14
37   Judges 16:19, 21, 25; Isaiah 53:3
38   Judges 16:30; 1 Corinthians 15:56-57

CHAPTER 5

CONVERSING IN SAMUEL, KINGS

Jonathan began to sing a hymn of praise as they all continued to walk the road to Emmaus. Cleopas soon joined in, and the two men raised their voices unto the heavens.

Jesus waited until they were done singing and then asked, "Why do you sing this hymn of praise to God?"

Jonathan answered, "Teacher, we have been walking on this road now for some time, and we have come to understand the Scriptures in a much greater way than we understood them before we began this journey. We praise God for how You have served as the voice of God for us."

"Yes," agreed Cleopas. "As we said to You from the start, we perceive You to be a prophet."

Jesus stopped walking and stood still. Jonathan and Cleopas stopped a few steps in front of Him and looked back as Jesus stepped forward to be able to look straight into their eyes.

"The prophets," Jesus reflected, "certainly, they too, pointed to the Messiah in their prophecies. Indeed, Samuel points to a faithful priest to come when he prophesies, 'But I will raise up for Myself a faithful priest who will do according to what is in My heart and in My soul.'[1] The Son of God would

---

1   1 Samuel 2:35

"become a merciful and faithful high priest in things pertaining to God, to make propitiation for the sins of the people.'[2] The prophets point to the Messiah.

"This same Messiah, the Son of God Who can be seen, appears to Samuel in order to supply his prophetic ministry. 'The LORD appeared again at Shiloh, because the LORD revealed Himself to Samuel at Shiloh by the word of the LORD.'[3] Jesus is seen in the Prophets."

Jesus continued His discussion as it pertained to Samuel. "Samuel reflects Christ in that he serves, like Christ, as prophet, priest, and judge. He, then, also describes David as a type of Christ. He depicts David as the anointed king[4] who becomes the forerunner of Jesus, the messianic King. As was the Christ, David was born in Bethlehem, acted as a shepherd, became the ruler of Israel, and was rejected and put in danger.[5] Christ is the Descendent, the Root and the Offspring of David.[6] It is David who is promised an everlasting kingdom.[7] It is Christ, the Son of David,[8] Who sits upon the throne of David[9] and fulfills that promise. Yes, 'the Lord God will give Him the throne of His father David; and He will reign over the house of Jacob forever, and His kingdom will have no end.' Amen.

"These things pertaining to David as he signals the coming of the Messiah are expanded upon by other prophets," explained Jesus. "Nathan spoke to David and prophesied of the coming Messiah as it is known that the Christ would 'reign over the house of Jacob forever'[10] and so Nathan tells David that God 'will raise up your descendant after you, who will come forth from you, and I will establish his kingdom. He shall build a house for My name, and I will establish the throne of his kingdom forever.'[11] The prophet points to the

---

2   Hebrews 2:17
3   1 Samuel 3:21
4   1 Samuel 16:13
5   Psalm 22
6   Romans 1:3; Revelation 22:16; Isaiah 9:7
7   2 Samuel 7:16
8   Matthew 21:9
9   Isaiah 9:7; Luke 1:32
10   Luke 1:32-33
11   2 Samuel 7:12-13; Colossians 2:9; Colossians 1:19

kingdom of the coming Christ, Who will Himself be the House or Dwelling of God; that is, Him in whom 'all the fullness of Deity dwells in bodily form.' This prophecy certainly points to Christ. Christ has come!"

"What about David himself?" Cleopas probed. "What does he say about the Christ?"

"David speaks of Christ frequently. He calls Him the Rock. The Rock, of course, is Christ.[12] David says, 'The Lord is my rock and my fortress'[13] and 'My God, my rock, in whom I take refuge.'[14] He asks, 'And who is a rock, besides our God?'[15] He then proclaims, 'The Lord lives, and blessed be my rock; and exalted be God, the rock of my salvation.'[16] Then in one comprehensive declaration, David includes the Trinity while specifically describing the Son of God as the Rock. 'The Spirit of the Lord spoke by me, and His word was on my tongue.' The God of Israel said, 'The Rock of Israel spoke to me.'[17] The Rock of Israel, the Messiah, is seen in the Tanakh."

Jonathan tried to digest what he had heard from the Teacher. "So, Samuel explains, in a variety of ways, how Jesus is seen in the Tanakh."

"Yes." Jesus looked at him with an affirming glance. "In fact, it is Samuel who references 'the angel of the Lord' as One with Whom David speaks as they are by the threshing floor of Araunah. He describes this pre-incarnate appearance of Jesus, saying, 'And the angel of the LORD was by the threshing floor of Araunah the Jebusite. Then David spoke to the LORD when he saw the angel who was striking down the people.'[18] Yes, Jonathan. Samuel explains in a variety of ways how Jesus is seen in the Tanakh."

Jesus turned to Jonathan and asked, "What else would you like to see, Jonathan?"

"Who else in the Scriptures can be seen as a type of Christ?"

---

12   1 Corinthians 10:4
13   2 Samuel 22:2
14   2 Samuel 22:3
15   2 Samuel 22:32
16   2 Samuel 22:47
17   2 Samuel 23:2-3
18   2 Samuel 24:16-17

"Elisha is a type of Christ," answered Jesus. "Like Christ, he lives among the people and emphasizes victory and hope.[19] On the other hand, John the Baptist, is a type of Elijah.[20] Both men lived apart from the people and stressed judgment and repentance.[21] John the Baptist preceded the Messiah, and Elijah preceded Elisha, even as repentance precedes victory. Here we have a foreshadowing of the coming of the Messiah."

The majority of people walking on the road to Emmaus were walking in the opposite direction toward Jerusalem. Jesus inquired of the two men traveling with Him, "Why are all of these people going to Jerusalem?"

Cleopas responded first. "They are going to the temple."

"What is the temple?" Jesus curiously asked.

"Teacher, what are you asking?" Cleopas was obviously uncomfortable with the peculiar nature of such a question coming from Him Who had come to be their Teacher.

Jonathan felt the tension and looked to quash it by simply answering Jesus' question in the most matter-of-fact way. "Teacher, as you know, the temple is the house of God. It houses God's presence."

Jesus motioned for Jonathan and Cleopas to follow Him as He walked a few steps off the road and stopped in front of a tree. Jesus pointed to a small spider web that was constructed between the base of the tree and a small bush. Using both of His hands, He picked up a large rock and dropped it on the spider web. He asked rhetorically, "Can that house that is but a web contain that rock?"

"Of course not," Jonathan answered, still somewhat baffled by the entire mode of discourse that had just taken place.

"How much more then can a house built with hands not be able to contain the Creator of heaven and earth?" Jesus had now arrived at His point. "Even the builder of the temple, Solomon, showed his understanding of this truth when he said, 'But will God indeed dwell on the earth? Behold, heaven and the

---

19   2 Kings 4:42-44; Matthew 14:13-20
20   Matthew 11:14; 17:10-12; Luke 1:17
21   1 Kings 17:1; Mark 1:4

highest heaven cannot contain You, how much less this house which I have built!'[22] The Messiah spoke of the temple but only in order to explain that He Himself is the ultimate Temple.[23] Solomon and the temple point to the Messiah. Only He can house the presence of God since in Him 'all the fullness of deity dwells in bodily form.'[24] Jesus, the Temple of God, is clearly seen in the Tanakh."

The three men returned to the road and resumed their journey. Jesus looked up to the sky and, seemingly, pointed to the clouds. "Why were Enoch and Elijah taken up into Heaven?"

Jonathan offered an answer. "Enoch walked with God right into Heaven, and Elijah was taken up in a whirlwind."

"What greater event is yet to come that is pictured by these two scenarios?" Jesus continued to point at the clouds up in the sky.

Cleopas was beginning to figure out where Jesus might be going with all this. "When that incredible event happened early this morning in which Mary Magdalene came back from the tomb and reported to us that Jesus was risen, she also said that He proclaimed that He would ascend to the Father."[25]

"This is the greater event that the two lesser events point to," confirmed Jesus. "Elijah's going up in a whirlwind to Heaven is a type of Jesus' bodily ascension to Heaven.[26] In both cases, it is advantageous for them to go, since the result will be the pouring out of the Spirit in greater measure. When Elijah ascends, Elisha receives a double portion of the Spirit that was upon him.[27] When Jesus ascends, He pours out the Holy Spirt upon His followers.[28] Via Enoch and Elijah, Jesus' ascension and His sending of the Holy Spirit are seen in the Tanakh."

---

22   1 Kings 8:21
23   John 2:19-21
24   Colossians 2:9
25   John 20:17
26   Luke 24:51
27   2 Kings 2:9-11
28   John 16:7

CHAPTER 6
CONVERSING IN ISAIAH

Cleopas wanted to ask Jesus a question. "Which prophet spoke the most about the Messiah?"

Without hesitation, Jesus answered. "That would most certainly be Isaiah."

"Tell us some ways in which Isaiah points to Him," Jonathan pleaded.

"Isaiah prophesies regarding the Messiah's second coming. He declares, 'In that day the Branch of the LORD will be beautiful and glorious, and the fruit of the earth *will be* the pride and the adornment of the survivors of Israel. It will come about that he who is left in Zion and remains in Jerusalem will be called holy—everyone who is recorded for life in Jerusalem. When the Lord has washed away the filth of the daughters of Zion and purged the bloodshed of Jerusalem from her midst, by the spirit of judgment and the spirit of burning.'[1] Christ, Who is the Branch, speaks of the timing of His second coming, saying, 'When its branch has already become tender and puts forth its leaves' then He will be 'near, right at the door.'[2] In this way, the Messiah is seen in the Scriptures."

Speaking pensively, Jesus recounted, "Isaiah saw one of the most glorious pictures of God any man could ever see. In the midst of the vision, Isaiah proclaimed, 'I saw the Lord sitting on a throne, lofty and exalted, with the

---

1   Isaiah 4:2-4
2   Matthew 24:32-33

train of His robe filling the temple. Seraphim stood above Him, each having six wings: with two he covered his face, and with two he covered his feet, and with two he flew.' Isaiah then described how one seraphim called out to another and said, '*Holy, Holy, Holy, is the LORD of hosts, the whole earth is full of His glory.*' Isaiah's eyes had seen the King, the LORD of hosts, and his ears had heard the voice of the Lord, saying, 'Whom shall I send, and who will go for Us?'"[3]

"Who is 'Us'?" asked Cleopas.

"'Us' is God! 'Us' is the Trinity. Jesus is seen here. There is One Who is referred to as 'the Lord God, the Almighty, who was and who is and who is to come. He sits on His throne and is worshipped.[4] He is part of the divine 'Us.' He is Jesus. Jesus is seen by the prophet in this wondrous vision."

"That is literally breathtaking. No, I mean literally." Jonathan stopped, bent over, and put his hands on his knees as he tried to catch his breath.

Cleopas added, "Oh, what a glorious God we have!"

Jonathan, having caught his breath now, shouted, "Jesus is God! Glory be to God. Glory be to Jesus."

"Yes, my friends, He is glorious," agreed Jesus. "And He does glorious things. He is, for example, the great Physician, Who heals those who turn to Him.[5] And so, Isaiah goes on to prophesy as He points to the Messiah saying, 'They might see with their eyes, hear with their ears, understand with their hearts, and return and be healed.'[6] The glorious Messiah is seen in the Tanakh.

"Isaiah, more than any other prophet, points to Christ," Jesus reflected. "He references the history of Christ, the mission of Christ, and the titles of Christ. There is much to be shown to you. It might be helpful to take a short break from our travels and sit down under that tree up ahead.

---

3   Isaiah 6:1-3, 5, 8
4   Revelation 4:8-10
5   Luke 5:31-32; Acts 3:19
6   Isaiah 6:10

"We can make it as though we are in a small classroom," Jonathan said enthusiastically.

"And then the Teacher can teach," Cleopas added.

Jesus sat down under the tree. Jonathan and Cleopas then sat down so as to sit at His feet.

"With regard to the history of Christ," Jesus began, "Isaiah points to His birth when he writes, 'Therefore the Lord Himself will give you a sign: Behold, a virgin will be with child and bear a son, and she will call His name Immanuel.'[7] Here, we not only see a picture of Jesus' miraculous virgin birth, but we also see a declaration—'Immanuel' means 'God is with us'—of the incarnation and divinity of Jesus. Isaiah also points to the lineage of Jesus and His anointing. 'Then a shoot will spring from the stem of Jesse, and a branch from his roots will bear fruit. The Spirit of the Lord will rest on Him.'[8] Truly, Isaiah references the history of Christ.

"With regard to the mission of Christ, Isaiah points to Him as Illuminator when he writes, 'The people who walk in darkness will see a great light; those who live in a dark land, the light will shine on them.'[9] Isaiah also refers to Christ as Judge. 'And He will delight in the fear of the LORD, and He will not judge by what His eyes see, nor make a decision by what His ears hear; but with righteousness He will judge.'[10] In addition, Isaiah points to Christ as Reprover. 'But with righteousness He will judge the poor, and decide with fairness for the afflicted of the earth; and He will strike the earth with the rod of His mouth, and with the breath of His lips He will slay the wicked.'[11] Christ is also seen as Law-giver. Isaiah writes, 'He will not be disheartened or crushed until He has established justice in the earth; and the coastlands will wait expectantly for His law.'[12]

---

7   Isaiah 7:14; Matthew 1:23
8   Isaiah 11:1-2; Revelation 5:5; Matthew 3:16
9   Isaiah 9:2; Luke 1:79
10   Isaiah 11:3-4; John 2:25
11   Isaiah 11:4; Revelation 19:15
12   Isaiah 42:4; Matthew 12:18

"Isaiah, literally, goes on and on in his descriptions of Christ. He is seen as Liberator,[13] Burden-bearer,[14] Suffering Savior,[15] Sin-bearer,[16] and Intercessor.[17] Truly, Isaiah references the mission of Christ.

"With regard to the titles of Christ, Isaiah refers to Him, perhaps most profoundly, as Immanuel.[18] Then he identifies Him as Mighty God, Everlasting Father, and Prince of Peace.[19] Christ is also referred to as Righteous King,[20] Divine Servant,[21] Arm of the Lord,[22] Anointed Preacher,[23] and Mighty Savior.[24] Truly, Isaiah references the titles of Christ.

"And so, Isaiah, who is a writer of the Word of God, makes references throughout his book to Jesus, the Word of God.[25] Jesus fits all of these descriptions, matches all of these functions, and holds all of these titles. He is Immanuel. He is the Suffering Savior. He is Mighty God! He is all these things and so much more. He is the Alpha and Omega[26] and eventually you will see 'the summing up of all things in Christ.'[27]

"So, class," Jesus playfully inquired, "what is your response to all this?"

"Glory be to Christ!" both Cleopas and Jonathan shouted simultaneously. "He is truly the One Who was, Who is, and Who is to come."

"Teacher," continued Cleopas, "we know that much of Christ's ministry is directed toward the Gentiles. Does Isaiah mention this in any way at all?"

"It is true, Cleopas," Jesus acknowledged. "Christ did leave Nazareth to go and shine as a great light on the Gentiles.[28] Isaiah refers to His ministry in the

---

13 Isaiah 42:7; Matthew 20:34
14 Isaiah 53:4; John 19:7
15 Isaiah 53:5; 1 Corinthians 15:3
16 Isaiah 53:6; Hebrews 9:28
17 Isaiah 53:12; Mark 15:28
18 Isaiah 7:14; Matthew 1:23
19 Isaiah 9:6; Matthew 1:23
20 Isaiah 32:1; Matthew 21:5
21 Isaiah 42:1; Mark 1:11
22 Isaiah 53:1; John 12:38
23 Isaiah 61:1; Mark 1:38
24 Isaiah 63:1; Matthew 18:11
25 John 1:1
26 Revelation 22:13
27 Ephesians 1:9-10
28 Matthew 4:12-17

land of Zebulun and Naphtali and 'on the other side of Jordan, Galilee of the Gentiles.'[29] There, the prophet wrote, 'The people who walk in darkness will see a great light; those who live in a dark land, the light will shine on them.'[30] So, yes, Cleopas, Jesus' Gentile ministry is seen in the Tanakh.

Just then, a large group of pilgrims passed them by on the other side of the road. In one woman's arms was a baby. The baby began to cry as the mother passed him on to his father.

"Truly, Jesus came to us as a baby," pondered Cleopas.

"Yes," confirmed Jonathan. "He was born in Bethlehem."

Jesus nodded His head in agreement. "Not only was a child born to us, but Isaiah prophesied about His birth seven hundred years before it happened. Isaiah writes, 'For a child will be born to us, a son will be given to us; and the government will rest on His shoulders; and His name will be called Wonderful Counselor, Mighty God, Eternal Father, Prince of Peace. There will be no end to the increase of His government or of peace on the throne of David and over his kingdom, to establish it and to uphold it with justice and righteousness from then on and forevermore.'"[31]

Jesus summarized, "Indeed, the Messiah was born in the city of David,[32] and He claimed to be God and spoke of His eternal kingdom. He is God, the Son of God. He is pictured in the Tanakh."

"These things are truly incredible!" stammered Cleopas. "How could a man have said these things, and then they come to pass seven hundred years later? He could not have said them by accident. He would not have said them by his own invention, for it is too radical to refer to God as a baby. Surely, a man could be stoned for saying such things."

"It is almost scandalous when you think about it," proposed Jonathan. "How could it be so, unless . . ." Jonathan paused.

---

29   Isaiah 9:1
30   Isaiah 9:2
31   Isaiah 9:6-7
32   Luke 2:11

Jesus finished Jonathan's unsaid conclusion. "Unless it is so! Unless it is true, and God really spoke through the prophet. Unless God, Himself, really was born to us."

Cleopas actually got down on his knees right in the middle of the road, and as other travelers passed him by, he cried out, "These things are too wonderful for my ears. I am but a sinful man. Yet, He is not. No, Jesus is the Son of God, and He is truly seen in the Tanakh."

"Jesus is, indeed, the Son of God," Jesus declared about Himself, and yet the two men still did not know it was He. "God the Father declared this truth at Jesus' baptism as the Spirit descended and rested upon Him.[33] Isaiah saw this as well.[34]'Then a shoot will spring from the stem of Jesse, and a branch from his roots will bear fruit. The Spirit of the Lord will rest on Him, the spirit of wisdom and understanding, the spirit of counsel and strength, the spirit of knowledge and the fear of the Lord.'[35] Once again, Jesus is seen in the Prophets.

"Jesus is Him 'who is and who was and who is to come, the Almighty,'"[36] the Teacher said authoritatively. "Before He was born or even before Abraham was born, He is.[37] He was, and He is. He is the One Who walked the earth and executed His ministry, even being baptized. He was, and He is, and He is to come. Isaiah saw all these things. He saw His birth. He saw His baptism. And He saw His second coming."

"Show us this return of the Christ," Jonathan begged.

"Listen and see," Jesus directed. "Christ will return and when He does 'from His mouth comes a sharp sword, so that with it He may strike down the nations, and He will rule them with a rod of iron.'[38] Isaiah sees the return of Christ and proclaims, 'But with righteousness He will judge the

---

33   Matt 3:16-17
34   Isaiah 42:1; Isaiah 61:1
35   Isaiah 11:1-2
36   Revelation 1:8
37   John 8:58
38   Revelation 19:15

poor, and decide with fairness for the afflicted of the earth; and He will strike the earth with the rod of His mouth, and with the breath of His lips He will slay the wicked.'[39] 'Then that lawless one will be revealed whom the Lord will slay with the breath of His mouth and bring to an end by the appearance of His coming.'[40]

"The return of Christ will be described by one who says, 'And I saw heaven opened, and behold, a white horse, and He who sat on it is called Faithful and True, and in righteousness He judges and wages war . . . He treads the wine press of the fierce wrath of God, the Almighty. And on His robe and on His thigh He has a name written, King of kings, and Lord of lords.'[41] Long ago, Isaiah saw this and described the coming judgment of God when Christ returns, adding 'also righteousness will be the belt about His loins, and faithfulness the belt about His waist.'[42] In wondrous ways, through the prophet Isaiah, Jesus is seen in the Scriptures."

Suddenly, Cleopas' countenance fell.

"What is wrong, my brother?" Jonathan asked with sincere concern.

"Jesus was born. But He died."

Jesus reentered the conversation. "It is true that He died. But it is also true that He rose from the dead. You may not see that yet, but Isaiah certainly saw it long ago."

"Isaiah saw the resurrection?" Cleopas now said with a hint of hope in his voice.

"Yes, my friend. Jesus is seen by the prophet Isaiah as the One in Whom the nations will find hope[43] and the One Who is the descendent of David,[44] Who will rise from the dead to gain victory for all.[45] Isaiah writes, 'Then in that day the nations will resort to the root of Jesse, who will stand as a signal for the

---

39   Isaiah 11:4
40   2 Thessalonians 2:8
41   Revelation 19:11, 15-16
42   Isaiah 11:5
43   Matthew 12:21
44   Matthew 1:1; Psalm 132:11
45   John 3:16

peoples; and His resting place will be glorious.'[46] Jesus is seen in the Tanakh."
Jesus asked Cleopas, "Do you remember what the name 'Jesus' means?"

"It means 'God saves.'"

"Yes," agreed Jesus. "Jesus is the Savior.[47] That means that man has a problem,[48] and God has the solution.[49] God, in Christ, becomes man's Savior. Isaiah describes Christ in this way when he asserts that men will say, 'I will give thanks to You, O LORD; for although You were angry with me, your anger is turned away, and You comfort me. Behold, God is my salvation, I will trust and not be afraid; for the LORD GOD is my strength and song, and He has become my salvation.'[50] Jesus, the Savior, is seen in the Scriptures."

Still pondering the return of Christ, Jonathan requested, "Tell us more about His second coming."

"The return of Christ will be associated with the destruction of the great city, Babylon, along with the nations that with her committed acts of immorality deserving of God's wrath and judgment.[51] The sun, moon, and stars will be darkened.[52] Jesus will return with His army, the bride, to wage war against the nations and the devil.[53] Isaiah foresees this and writes, 'The oracle concerning Babylon which Isaiah the son of Amoz saw . . . I have even called My mighty warriors, My proudly exulting ones, to execute My anger. A sound of tumult on the mountains, like that of many people! A sound of the uproar of kingdoms, of nations gathered together! The LORD of hosts is mustering the army for battle. They are coming from a far country, from the farthest horizons, the LORD and His instruments of indignation, to destroy the whole land. Wail, for the day of the LORD is near! It will come as destruction from the Almighty . . . Behold, the day of the LORD is

---

46   Isaiah 11:10
47   Luke 2:11
48   Romans 3:23
49   John 3:17
50   Isaiah 12:1-2
51   Revelation 18:1-10
52   Revelation 8:12
53   Revelation 19:7-8, 14, 19; Malachi 4:2-3

coming, cruel, with fury and burning anger, to make the land a desolation and He will exterminate its sinners from it. For the stars of heaven and their constellations will not flash forth their light; the sun will be dark when it rises and the moon will not shed its light. Thus I will punish the world for its evil and the wicked for their iniquity; I will also put an end to the arrogance of the proud and abase the haughtiness of the ruthless.'[54] The return of Christ is seen in the Scriptures."

Jesus continued. "Isaiah sees more things associated with these latter times. He foreshadows the final and complete authority given to Jesus. 'Then I will set the key of the house of David on his shoulder, when he opens no one will shut, when he shuts no one will open.'[55] It will be seen that, in fact, this is the authority given to Jesus. In latter times, it will be written to the angel of the church in Philadelphia, 'He who is holy, who is true, who has the key of David, who opens and no one will shut, and who shuts and no one opens.'[56] Jesus—He who was, and who is, and who is to come—is seen in the Scriptures."

"It will be told to you later," explained Jesus, "that when the Lord returns there will be a New Jerusalem and that 'the city has no need of the sun or of the moon to shine on it, for the glory of God has illumined it, and its lamp is the Lamb.'[57] Of this, Isaiah saw ahead and wrote, 'Then the moon will be abashed and the sun ashamed, for the Lord of hosts will reign on Mount Zion and in Jerusalem, and His glory will be before His elders.'[58] The light of the Lamb of God, the Messiah, is pictured in the Tanakh."

Jonathan positioned himself behind Cleopas and placed his hands upon his shoulders. Playfully, he propositioned, "Oh that we could see the things that Isaiah saw."

Jesus interjected, "Perhaps you will. Perhaps you will."

---

54 Isaiah 13:1-11
55 Isaiah 22:22
56 Revelation 3:7
57 Revelation 21:23
58 Isaiah 24:23

"How can we see?" asked Cleopas with a clear bit of doubt in the tone of his voice.

"You will see because Jesus came that you might see. In fact, the Son of God removed the veil that keeps people from seeing God.[59] Ultimately, God will give the victory as death is swallowed up.[60] Isaiah prophesies about this when he writes, 'The Lord of hosts will prepare a lavish banquet for all peoples on this mountain . . . and on this mountain He will swallow up the covering which is over all peoples, even the veil which is stretched over all nations. He will swallow up death for all time.'[61] The work of the Son of God is seen in the Tanakh."

Jesus pointed to a large stone on the side of the road. "Jonathan, what is that?"

"A stone."

"Is it the most important stone?"

"No. The chief cornerstone is the most important stone."

"Why is that?"

"Because it is from the chief cornerstone that everything else derives its design. The chief cornerstone is indispensable. It is what everything else is built on."

Jesus smiled. "Well said, Jonathan! Jesus is that Cornerstone. Isaiah prophesies of Him. 'Behold, I am laying in Zion a stone, a tested stone, a costly cornerstone for the foundation, firmly placed. He who believes in it will not be disturbed.'[62] Jesus is that Cornerstone, and he who believes in Him will not be disturbed.[63] Jesus is seen in the Scriptures."

"What drew you to that Cornerstone, Jonathan?" Jesus inquired.

"Initially, His miraculous healings. No one had ever done all that He did."

---

59   Matthew 27:51
60   1 Corinthians 15:54-57
61   Isaiah 25:6-8
62   Isaiah 28:16
63   1 Corinthians 3:11; 1 Peter 2:4-6; John 3:16

"Isaiah envisioned His healing ministry.[64] 'They will see the glory of the Lord, the majesty of our God, He will save you. Then the eyes of the blind will be opened and the ears of the deaf will be unstopped. Then the lame will leap like a deer, and the tongue of the mute will shout for joy.'[65] Jesus' healing ministry is seen in the Prophets."

Someone down the hill, just off the road, was yelling quite loudly. Jesus cupped his hand around his ear and leaned toward the sound. "What is that?"

"Someone who wants others to hear him . . . that's for sure!" Jonathan chuckled.

"And who might this be?" Jesus asked. "This voice that is calling, 'Clear the way for the LORD in the wilderness; make smooth in the desert a highway for our God. Let every valley be lifted up, and every mountain and hill be made low; and let the rough ground become a plain, and the rugged terrain a broad valley; Then the glory of the LORD will be revealed, and all flesh will see it together; for the mouth of the LORD has spoken.'"[66]

"That sounds like John the Baptist," offered Jonathan. "He lived in the desert and preached repentance to usher in the launch of Jesus' ministry."

"It is a very good description of John the Baptist—'the voice of one calling in the wilderness.'[67] And yet, that description was actually prophesied by Isaiah seven hundred years earlier. Jesus' ministry is pointed to in the Tanakh."

Just then, a stray sheep walked across the road. Jesus shepherded the sheep back to where she had come from. A shepherd came running up the hill calling to Jesus, "Thank you, sir; that is my sheep." Jesus gave one final nudge to the sheep as it ran down the hill toward its shepherd, and they were reunited.

"Jesus is the Good Shepherd.[68] Isaiah writes about Him, saying, 'Here is your God! Behold, the Lord God will come with might, with His arm ruling for Him. Behold, His reward is with Him and His recompense before Him.

---

64   Matthew 15:30; Matthew 11:5
65   Isaiah 35:2-6
66   Isaiah 40:3-5
67   Matthew 3:1-3; Matthew 11:10
68   John 10:14

Like a shepherd He will tend His flock, in His arm He will gather the lambs and carry them in His bosom; He will gently lead the nursing ewes.'[69] The Good Shepherd is pictured in the Tanakh."

Jesus continued. "When Jesus was baptized and transfigured, God the Father referred to Him as His beloved Son, the chosen one who is the Spirit-anointed Servant in Whom God is well-pleased.[70] Isaiah illustrated it this way: 'Behold, My Servant, whom I uphold; My chosen one in whom My soul delights. I have put My Spirit upon Him; He will bring forth justice to the nations.'[71] Again, Jesus is put forth in the Prophets."

Near the road was a marshy area. Travelers were resting their weary feet and refreshing themselves with some water. Jesus motioned to His companions. "Come, let us take some water."

The men sat down in front of a row of reeds. "Be careful, Jonathan," Jesus warned. "That reed next to you is bruised and shall not be broken."

"Who concerns himself with bruised reeds?"

"The Messiah. He who brings forth justice on the earth and justice to the Gentiles.[72] He who is humble and meek[73] and Who searches for the lost sheep.[74] Isaiah describes this when he writes, 'He will not cry out or raise His voice, nor make His voice heard in the street. A bruised reed He will not break and a dimly burning wick He will not extinguish; He will faithfully bring forth justice.'[75] The justice of the Messiah is to save the lost.[76] Jesus is seen in the Tanakh."

The three men were sitting in close proximity to many other people. They could not help but overhear them talking. Jonathan whispered to Cleopas, "There seem to be people here from other lands. Their language is not ours."

69　Isaiah 40:9-11
70　Matthew 3:16-17; Luke 9:35
71　Isaiah 42:1
72　Matthew 12:15-21
73　Matthew 11:29
74　John 10:11
75　Isaiah 42:2-3
76　John 3:17

"Messiah is the Light to the nations," Jesus firmly declared. Isaiah prophesies, 'I am the LORD, I have called you in righteousness, I will also hold you by the hand and watch over you, and I will appoint you as a covenant to the people, as a light to the nations.'[77] After Christ is born, Simeon comes into the temple; and after seeing Him, he prays to God, "For my eyes have seen Your salvation, which You have prepared in the presence of all peoples, a light of revelation to the gentiles, and the glory of Your people Israel.'[78] The coming of the light to the nations is predicted in the Scriptures."

Jesus cupped His hands together and collected water, letting it rest in His hands. He just stared at it for a while. Then He lifted His hands above His head. Still holding the water, He opened His hands so that it spilled out onto His head and ran down his face and onto His shoulders.

"Christ will pour out His Spirit upon you as He said of the Spirit, 'If I go, I will send Him to you.'[79] Surely, Isaiah points to this when he writes, 'For I will pour out water on the thirsty land and streams on the dry ground; I will pour out My Spirit on your offspring and My blessing on your descendants.'[80] The Messiah is seen in the Scriptures.

"Christ Jesus is the only true God, Who will appear as the Redeemer for those who are 'looking for the blessed hope and the appearing of the glory of our great God and Savior, Christ Jesus, who gave Himself for us to redeem us.'[81] He is the first and the last,[82] and He is the Rock.[83] Surely, Isaiah describes Him when he writes, 'Thus says the Lord, the King of Israel and his Redeemer, the Lord of hosts: I am the first and I am the last, and there is no God besides Me. Who is like Me? . . . Is there any God besides Me, or is there any other Rock?'[84] What a description of the Christ! Jesus is seen in the Prophets."

---

77   Isaiah 42:6
78   Luke 2:30-32
79   John 16:7; Acts 2:1-4
80   Isaiah 44:3
81   Titus 2:13-14
82   Revelation 22:13, 16
83   1 Corinthians 10:4
84   Isaiah 44:6-8

Jesus rose up and began to walk back to the road. "Come, my fellow travelers. Let us steadfastly set our faces to go to Emmaus."

Jonathan and Cleopas followed Him, and they resumed their journey.

"You know, Jonathan and Cleopas . . . " Jesus pointed straight ahead. "The Messiah was obedient to go to the cross[85] and, thus, 'He steadfastly set His face to go to Jerusalem.'[86] Isaiah describes this when he refers to the Messiah's words, 'And I was not disobedient, nor did I turn back . . . therefore, I have set My face like flint.'[87]

"Isaiah goes on to prophesy about the way in which they scourged Him prior to the crucifixion as they spit in His face and slapped and hit Him with their fists.[88] 'I gave My back to those who strike Me, and My cheeks to those who pluck out the beard; I did not cover My face from humiliation and spitting.'[89] The Messiah is seen in the Scriptures."

"Three days ago, we saw what Isaiah saw seven hundred years ago," Cleopas lamented. "We saw Him as He walked up that hill with His cross. His back was stripped of its flesh. His head was disheveled. His hair was drenched in blood. His face was marred. It is unthinkable. But it happened. We saw it."

"And Isaiah saw it as well," repeated Jonathan. "What else, Master, did Isaiah see?"

"The Son of God is God Who has been revealed to all men[90] so that all may see the salvation of God.[91] Isaiah describes the incarnation and mission of the Messiah this way: 'The Lord has bared His holy arm in the sight of all the nations, that all the ends of the earth may see the salvation of our God.'[92]

85　Philippians 2:8
86　Luke 9:51, NKJV
87　Isaiah 50:5, 7, NASB
88　Matthew 26:67; Matthew 27:26
89　Isaiah 50:6
90　2 Timothy 1:10
91　Mark 13:10
92　Isaiah 52:10

"The Messiah is the suffering servant[93] who is brutally tortured[94] for the forgiveness of the sins of all the people[95] that they might know Him.[96] In so doing, the Messiah is highly exalted so that at the name of Jesus every knee would bow.[97] Isaiah saw this and wrote, 'Behold, My servant will prosper, He will be high and lifted up and greatly exalted. Just as many were astonished at you, *My people*, so His appearance was marred more than any man and His form more than the sons of men. Thus He will sprinkle many nations, Kings will shut their mouths on account of Him; For what had not been told them they will see, And what they had not heard they will understand.'[98] These things, and much more, Isaiah saw."

"Halleluiah!" shouted Jonathan.

"Praise God, Who reveals Himself," Cleopas added.

Jonathan looked at Cleopas. Then He looked at Jesus. He looked up in the sky with his jaw dropped as though he, himself, had just received a revelation.

"Revelation?" asked Jesus.

"Yes," clamored Jonathan. "This is the business of God. His business is to reveal Himself. He is not a tentmaker, nor a tax-gatherer, nor a merchant. None of those are His profession. He is in the business of revelation. And He is very good at it."

"And so, Jonathan, you are seeing Jesus in the Scriptures?" Jesus half-asked and half-stated.

"Yes, Teacher. Show us more."

"Messiah came as a common man.[99] Isaiah says, 'To whom has the arm of the Lord been revealed? For He grew up before Him like a tender shoot, and like a root out of parched ground; He has no stately form or majesty that we

---

93   1 Peter 2:21
94   Matthew 26:67; Matthew 27:28-31
95   1 Corinthians 15:3
96   John 14:7; John 1:18
97   Philippians 2:8-11
98   Isaiah 52:13-15
99   Philippians 2:8

should look upon Him, nor appearance that we should be attracted to Him.'[100] Isaiah prophesied of the way in which Christ was rejected[101] and mocked as His enemies prepared Him for the cross[102] 'He was despised and forsaken of men, a man of sorrows and acquainted with grief; and like one from whom men hide their face He was despised, and we did not esteem Him.'[103] Yes, Jonathan, God's business prospers as He paints vivid pictures of Christ in the Prophets over and over again."

"What is the most precious piece He has in His business?" Jonathan asked as though he were picturing a booth with a sign, "Pieces of Revelation," and individual pieces highlighted in the front shelf of the store.

"Precious is the revelation of the salvation of God that He provides by His own suffering; His substitutionary death so that you may live. Isaiah prophesied of Messiah's divine healing ministry[104] that is ultimately manifested in spiritual healing.[105] Isaiah foresees this and writes, 'Surely our griefs He Himself bore, and our sorrows He carried; yet we ourselves esteemed Him stricken, smitten of God, and afflicted. But He was pierced through for our transgressions, He was crushed for our iniquities; the chastening for our well-being fell upon Him, and by His scourging we are healed.'[106] Again, Christ is seen in the Scriptures as God continues to build His business; the business of revelation."

Jesus continued. "Christ is the Suffering Servant because He is the Good Shepherd. Those whom the Good Shepherd came for are like lost sheep,[107] and thus, the Shepherd must lay down His life for them[108] by taking the penalty due them.[109] Isaiah declared this, 'All of us like sheep have gone astray, each

---

100 Isaiah 53:1-2
101 John 1:11
102 Matthew 27:29-31
103 Isaiah 53:3
104 Matthew 8:16-17
105 Matthew 9:5-6; 1 Peter 2:24; Romans 5:8
106 Isaiah 53:4-5
107 Luke 15:4
108 John 10:11
109 John 1:29; 2 Corinthians 5:21

of us has turned to his own way; but the Lord has caused the iniquity of us all to fall on Him.'[110]

"What a Savior!" Cleopas declared.

"What a revelation!" Jonathan added. "Surely, Jesus is seen in the Scriptures."

"You were there three days ago when that Good Shepherd laid down His life for the sheep," Jesus reminded Cleopas. "What did the Shepherd do as He was being tortured? Did He try to get away? Did He fight back?"

Cleopas stopped for a moment. His gaze seemed to go far away as though he were suddenly somewhere else. "As He stood before His accusers, the Christ did not open His mouth.[111] As He was being prepared for crucifixion—to the amazement of His torturers—He remained silent before His prosecutors.[112] Even 'while being reviled, He did not revile in return; while suffering, He uttered no threats.'"[113]

"Isaiah, seven hundred years before the crucifixion of Christ, described that very scene that you viewed, Cleopas, in this way: 'He was oppressed and He was afflicted, yet He did not open His mouth; like a lamb that is led to slaughter, and like a sheep that is silent before its shearers, so He did not open His mouth.'[114] What you saw three days ago, Isaiah saw seven hundred years ago.

"He saw the Messiah's substitutionary death.[115] 'He was cut off out of the land of the living, for the transgression of My people to whom the stroke was due.'[116] In addition to this, Isaiah prophesied concerning the role of the wealthy Nicodemus and Joseph of Arimathea[117] in the death and burial of the Christ as He wrote, 'Yet He was with a rich man in His death.'[118] Christ is seen in the Tanakh.

---

110   Isaiah 53:6
111   Psalm 38:12-14
112   Matthew 26:63; Matthew 27:12-14
113   1 Peter 2:23
114   Isaiah 53:7
115   John 1:29
116   Isaiah 53:8
117   John 19:38-42
118   Isaiah 53:9

"Cleopas, you were there three days ago," Jesus confirmed.

"Yes, Teacher. Both Jonathan and I were there at that God-forsaken event."

"What you speak is true in the most confounding way. It was a God-forsaken event."

"Who was forsaken by God?"

"Jesus was forsaken. God forsook God. Confounding! The result of sin is death or spiritual separation.[119] When Jesus became sin[120] on the cross, He was, paradoxically, separated from Himself. Thus, He cried out, 'My God, My God why have You forsaken Me?'"[121]

"How about another confounding truth?" Jesus offered.

"Go ahead," Jonathan and Cleopas answered almost simultaneously.

"Who put Jesus to death on the cross?"

"The Romans," Cleopas barked back with a clear sense of anger in his voice.

"No. It is the Jewish leaders who are the most to blame," Jonathan clarified.

"No," Cleopas paused as he reevaluated his answer. "It was my sin and the sin of all mankind."

Jesus reentered the discussion. "More foundationally, and thus, more exhaustively, the One Who put Jesus to death is God. Confounding! Inasmuch as the Son of God and the Father are One, God paradoxically put Himself to death. As Isaiah prophesied, 'The Lord was pleased to crush Him, putting Him to grief.'[122] This is why Jesus cried out from the cross, 'My God, My God why have You forsaken Me?' As much as the reality of the Trinity yields a sense of paradox relative to God's unity—for example, the idea that God is with God[123]—it also yields a sense of paradox relative to His separation seen on the cross as God is separated from God."

"How could Jesus have endured this?" Cleopas said as if he was complaining.

---

119   Romans 6:23
120   2 Corinthians 5:21
121   Matthew 27:46; Psalm 22:1
122   Isaiah 53:10
123   John 1:1

"Love," Jesus stated so matter-of-factly that the speaking of that word almost seemed to shake the ground. "He endured all of it because of His love[124] and because of 'the joy set before Him.'[125] Isaiah prophesied, 'If He would render Himself as a guilt offering, He will see His offspring, He will prolong His days, and the good pleasure of the Lord will prosper in His hand. As a result of the anguish of His soul, He will see it and be satisfied; by His knowledge the Righteous One, My Servant, will justify the many, as He will bear their iniquities.'[126] Oh, how the Son of God is seen in the Scriptures!"

A bit of a raucous arose on the other side of the road. It was clear what was happening. A man had been caught in the act of stealing from a roadside stand, and he was being drug by a mob to the feet of the merchant whose stand it was. "That robber will surely be put to death," announced Cleopas.

"Perhaps he will die next to Christ," Jesus surmised.

Suddenly, Cleopas remembered. "Oh, that is a terrible picture."

Jesus began, "It is a trustworthy statement that 'the Son of Man did not come to be served, but to serve, and to give His life a ransom for many.'[127] When He was put to death, He was 'numbered with the transgressors'[128] and placed next to the robbers and criminals.[129] Truly, He interceded for one of them and told him, 'Today you shall be with Me in Paradise.'[130] Isaiah the prophet described these things when he wrote, 'Because He poured out Himself to death, and was numbered with the transgressors; yet He Himself bore the sin of many, and interceded for the transgressors.'[131] Amazingly, Christ and His crucifixion is seen in detailed ways in the Tanakh."

"So, Jesus actually died for thieves and robbers?" Cleopas muttered in a questioning tone of voice.

---

124 John 3:16
125 Hebrews 12:2
126 Isaiah 53:10-11
127 Matthew 20:28
128 Mark 15:28
129 John 18:40; Luke 23:33
130 Luke 23:43
131 Isaiah 53:12

"Not quite, Cleopas," Jesus responded quickly. "Christ actually died for everyone."

"Even the Gentiles?"

"Yes, my friend, even the Gentiles."

"Why?"

"Why? Because God so loved the world. You know, Cleopas, the prophet Isaiah, from long ago, describes this when He writes, 'I will also make You a light of the nations so that My salvation may reach to the end of the earth.'[132] Then he writes, "Peace, peace to him who is far and to him who is near . . . and I will heal him.'[133] Through the Son of God both Jew and Gentile have their 'access in one Spirit to the Father.'[134] Indeed, Christ's mission is seen in the ancient Scriptures."

"And Christ's mission is the mission to provide salvation?" Jonathan clarified.

"It is what Christ came to do," confirmed Jesus.

"Why must Christ provide salvation?" Cleopas countered.

Jesus paused. "Because man cannot provide it for himself. Christ not only does provide salvation, but He also must provide salvation. There is no other way."

"Do the prophets see it this way?" Jonathan inquired.

"Isaiah the prophet saw the Son of God and His salvation. As he addressed the lack of justice that existed due to the want of payment for sin, he wrote, 'And He saw that there was no man, and was astonished that there was no one to intercede.'[135] Jesus' plan of salvation is based on the fact that man cannot save himself.[136] And so, Isaiah wrote, 'Then His own arm brought salvation to Him, and His righteousness upheld Him.'[137] God must provide salvation

---

132 Isaiah 49:6
133 Isaiah 57:19
134 Ephesians 2:11-18
135 Isaiah 59:16
136 Galatians 2:21
137 Galatians 2:21

Himself.[138] Jesus is the author of salvation.[139] Herein, Jesus is certainly seen in the Scriptures."

Jonathan again felt the need to recap what was just said. "And so, the Messiah has come because He had to come? There was no other way."

Jesus took the opportunity to personalize the reality of this truth for both Jonathan and Cleopas. "You are dead in your sins. Can a dead man climb a hill? Since you cannot climb up the hill to God, God, then, climbs down the hill to you."

Jesus stepped off the road and approached a steep hill. Jonathan and Cleopas stood and watched. Jesus then scampered down the hill, and once He arrived at the bottom, He shouted up to the two men.

"Know this, my friends. God loves you so much that He would leave the heights and luxuries of His abode above and lower Himself to become as one of you.[140] He did this because you could not climb."

"Can we still not climb?" Cleopas asked hopefully.

"Once He climbs to you and you receive Him, He makes you alive so that you can climb with Him. You climb because He first climbed to you."[141]

"Will we even be able to climb up to the new heavens and the new earth at the end of the age?"

"Yes, many will," Jesus said elatedly. "Christ will return to usher in the new heavens and the new earth. It will have 'no temple in it, for the Lord God the Almighty and the Lamb are its temple. And the city has no need of the sun or of the moon to shine on it, for the glory of God has illumined it, and its lamp is the Lamb. The nations will walk by its light, and the kings of the earth will bring their glory into it.'[142] Long ago, Isaiah saw Jesus in this great new city and wrote, 'Arise, shine; for your light has come, and the glory of the Lord has risen upon you. For behold, darkness will cover the

---

138 Isaiah 59:20
139 Hebrews 2:10
140 Philippians 2:5-8
141 1 John 4:19
142 Revelation 21:22-24

earth and deep darkness the peoples; but the Lord will rise upon you and His glory will appear upon you. Nations will come to your light, and kings to the brightness of your rising.'[143] Jesus and the new heavens and new earth are seen in the Tanakh."

Jesus continued. "It is a wondrous truth that when Messiah returns, there will be a new heaven and a new earth. It will be inhabited by the saved ones, who are righteous, and there will be no violence or mourning, but only peace and praise. The sun and moon will no longer need to cast their light, for Jesus Christ, the Lamb, will be the Light.[144] Isaiah sees this vividly and declares God's words, 'I will make peace your administrators and righteousness your overseers. Violence will not be heard again in your land, nor devastation or destruction within your borders; but you will call your walls salvation, and your gates praise. No longer will you have the sun for light by day, nor for brightness will the moon give you light; but you will have the Lord for an everlasting light, and your God for your glory . . . and the days of your mourning will be over.'[145] What a wonderful picture Isaiah saw of Jesus!"

"Yes!" Cleopas said with conviction, "I want to go to that amazing place that needs no sun. May I go, Teacher?"

"Indeed, you may," Jesus responded invitingly. "Just make sure you let the Son climb down the mountain to you."

"Know this," added Jesus. "The Messiah, the Word of God, will return wearing a robe dipped in blood.[146] Isaiah saw this second coming of the Word of God, Who was wearing a robe dipped in blood. He wrote, 'Their lifeblood is sprinkled on My garments . . . So My own arm brought salvation to Me.'[147] Isaiah saw the Word of God."

"Please tell us more about the new heavens and the new earth," Jonathan pleaded.

---

143 Isaiah 60:1-3
144 Revelation 21
145 Isaiah 60:17-20
146 Revelation 19:13
147 Isaiah 63:3, 5

"Isaiah prophesies that the new heavens and the new earth will be created when Jesus returns.[148] It is full of peace and joy[149] and has no mourning.[150] The old earth will be judged by fire,[151] but those who have remained true to the Messiah will gather from all the nations.[152] To those who are far off from Isaiah, that same picture will be revealed.[153] Isaiah paints a picture of the Messiah and the new heavens and new earth."

"Isaiah was certainly a seer," declared Jonathan with a sense of awe in his voice.

"Seers, of course, see things!" Cleopas declared. "Isaiah saw Christ."

"Yes," Jesus agreed. "He saw many things about the Christ. He saw His ministry of preaching the Gospel to the poor, casting out demons, and healing the sick.[154] Perhaps, most significantly, He saw the substitutionary death of the Son of God, Who by His mercy, bore the punishment of the people He loved and saved them from their sins. Isaiah wrote, 'So He became their Savior. In all their affliction He was afflicted, and the angel of His presence saved them; in His love and in His mercy He redeemed them, and He lifted them and carried them.'[155] Yes, Isaiah saw!"

---

148   Isaiah 65:17; Isaiah 66:22
149   Isaiah 65:18, 25
150   Isaiah 65:19
151   Isaiah 66:15-16, 24
152   Isaiah 66:18-20
153   Revelation 21; 18:8; Mark 9:43-48
154   Isaiah 61:1-2; Matthew 11:4-5
155   Isaiah 63:8-9

CHAPTER 7

CONVERSING IN JEREMIAH, EZEKIEL

Up ahead was a market. Various merchants were selling their wares, and there was even a potter who was at work shaping a bowl on his potter's wheel.

"Look at the potter," Jesus said. "He controls the wheel, and thus, the vessel."

"Yes," Jonathan surmised. "He can either make it or break it."

"In the end times, Jesus takes the role of a Potter Who breaks His vessel to pieces.[1] The picture of God the Potter is foreshadowed by Jeremiah. 'Can I not, O house of Israel, deal with you as this potter does? Behold, like the clay in the potter's hand, so are you in My hand, O house of Israel.'[2] Then he prophesies, 'Just so will I break this people and this city, even as one breaks a potter's vessel.'[3] Herein, Jesus, the One Who is to come, the Almighty,[4] is seen in the Scriptures."

Jesus continued looking all around at that which surrounded them. He locked in on someone who was quite a distance away.

"Do you see that shepherd out in the field?" Jesus asked Jonathan.

"Yes, Teacher. And we know that Jesus is the Good Shepherd."

---

1   Revelation 2:27
2   Jeremiah 18:6
3   Jeremiah 19:11
4   Revelation 1:8

"Jesus is the Good Shepherd Who saves His flock of sheep.[5] He is the righteous Branch raised up from David as King of the Jews, and He is the One who is revealed as God's righteousness.[6] Jeremiah paints the same picture of Him six hundred years earlier when he prophesies, 'Then I Myself will gather the remnant of My flock out of all the countries where I have driven them and bring them back to their pasture, and they will be fruitful and multiply . . . Behold, the days are coming when I will raise up for David a righteous Branch; and He will reign as king and act wisely and do justice and righteousness in the land. In His days Judah will be saved, and Israel will dwell securely; and this is His name by which He will be called, 'The Lord our righteousness.'[7] A clear painting of Jesus is seen in the Prophets."

The three men passed by a woman on the side of the road who was weeping and being comforted by her friends. Jesus remarked, "Jeremiah saw a heartbreaking thing. Herod, in trying to kill Jesus, killed all males 'from two years old and under.'[8] Jeremiah prophesied, 'A voice is heard in Ramah, lamentation and bitter weeping. Rachel is weeping for her children; she refuses to be comforted for her children, because they are no more.'[9] Jeremiah saw what happened to Jesus even when He was a baby."

Jesus stopped for a moment. He bent down and drew in the dirt.

"Why do you draw that arrow in the dirt?" Cleopas questioned as he bent down to get a closer look.

"The arrow points to something, and it points away from something," Jesus replied as He drew an "x" before the arrow and another "x" after the arrow.

Jesus continued. "The first "x" that is before the arrow is the Old Covenant, and the "x" that the arrow is pointing to is the New Covenant. It is true. The New Covenant is seen in the Old Covenant, for the New Covenant continues,

5   John 10:11-16
6   Matthew 2:2; Romans 1:17
7   Jeremiah 23:3, 5-6
8   Matthew 2:18
9   Jeremiah 31:15

completes, and fulfills the Old Covenant. The Old Covenant points ahead to the New Covenant because it is consistent with it and expectant of it."

Jesus rose up and began to walk down the road again. "Christ is the Mediator of a New Covenant that both reflects on and fulfills the previous covenants made with Adam and Able, Noah, Abraham, Moses, and David. Jeremiah foresees this New Covenant and its Mediator and writes, *'Behold, days are coming, declares the LORD, when I will make a new covenant with the house of Israel and with the house of Judah . . . I will put My law within them and on their heart I will write it; and I will be their God, and they shall be My people . . . for I will forgive their iniquity, and their sin I will remember no more.'*[10] The Christ of the New Covenant is the Christ of the Old Covenant. Thus, Christ is seen in the Tanakh."

Jonathan began clapping his hands almost as though he were giving some sort of ovation to the Teacher. "Christ is seen in the Tanakh. He is seen throughout the Tanakh. And He is seen in so many different ways."

Cleopas entered in. "Is the Christ even seen in some of the strange visions that such Prophets as Ezekiel had?"

"Listen and see," Jesus whispered. "Christ and the fullness of His ministry are represented by the four living beings that Ezekiel saw[11] and that will be seen when Christ returns.[12] Each of the four beings had four faces. The face of a man represents Jesus the Man,[13] the incarnation. The face of a lion represents Jesus the King,[14] as is consistent with the books of the Torah and the gift of gold given by the magi at Jesus' birth.[15] The face of an ox or bull represents Jesus the Priest,[16] as is consistent with the teaching of the Writings and the gift of frankincense—used in the temple ministry—given by the

---

10   Jeremiah 31:31, 33-34
11   Ezekiel 1:5-6, 10
12   Revelation 4:7
13   Philippians 2:7-8
14   Matthew 2:2
15   Matthew 2:11
16   Hebrews 3:1

magi at Jesus' birth. The face of an eagle represents Jesus the Prophet,[17] as is consistent with the books of the Prophets and the gift of myrrh—used for embalming, prophesying Jesus' death and burial—given by the magi at Jesus' birth. Jesus, in the four majestic beings, is seen as Divine King, Priest, and Prophet Who has come as a Man. Yes, Cleopas, the Christ is even seen in a strange vision had by the prophet Ezekiel."

Jesus continued to mine the depths of Ezekiel's visions.

"Ezekiel sees a majestic vision of God, Who is said to have the appearance of a Man. 'Now above the expanse that was over their heads there was something resembling a throne, like lapis lazuli in appearance; and on that which resembled a throne, high up, was a figure with the appearance of a man. Then I noticed from the appearance of His loins and upward something like glowing metal that looked like fire all around within it, and from the appearance of His loins and downward I saw something like fire; and there was a radiance around Him. As the appearance of the rainbow in the clouds on a rainy day, so was the appearance of the surrounding radiance. Such was the appearance of the likeness of the glory of the Lord. And when I saw it, I fell on my face.'[18] Who is this Man Who appears as God? He is the only One Who is both God and Man. He is Jesus! Here is a pre-incarnate appearance of Christ in the Scriptures."

Jesus bent over and picked up a twig. He pointed toward the hills. "Do you see the stately cedars reaching to the sky? How wonderful it is that this small twig can become that splendid cedar."

Jesus threw the twig back on the ground. "Even as the Messiah is described as the Branch by Isaiah,[19] He is also portrayed by Ezekiel as a tender twig that becomes a stately cedar on a lofty mountain. 'I will also take a sprig from the lofty top of the cedar and set it out; I will pluck from the topmost of its young twigs a tender one and I will plant it on a high and lofty mountain. On

17   Acts 3:22
18   Ezekiel 1:26-28
19   Isaiah 11:1

the high mountain of Israel I will plant it, that it may bring forth boughs and bear fruit and become a stately cedar. And birds of every kind will nest under it; they will nest in the shade of its branches. All the trees of the field will know that I am the Lord; I bring down the high tree, exalt the low tree, dry up the green tree and make the dry tree flourish. I am the Lord; I have spoken, and I will perform it.'[20] The Messiah, the humble One, becomes the highly exalted One.[21] The smallest of twigs or seeds becomes the largest of 'all the garden plants and forms large branches so that the birds of the air can nest under its shade.'[22] Messiah is seen in the Tanakh.

"The coming of the humble Messiah Who will eventually be exalted[23] is depicted by Ezekiel when he prophesies, 'Remove the turban and take off the crown; this will no longer be the same. Exalt that which is low and abase that which is high. A ruin, a ruin, a ruin, I will make it. This also will be no more until He comes whose right it is, and I will give it to Him.'[24] He has come, and He will come again. Ezekiel points to Him."

"Should we take a break and rest our feet a bit?" Cleopas asked, sounding like he was both inviting the other two and at the same time begging them.

"Come, let us rest," Jesus affirmed. The three men went and sat under a tree.

"Master, teach us about the Good Shepherd," Jonathan prompted.

"Jesus, the true Shepherd, delivers, feeds, and judges His flock. He delivers His sheep from the false shepherds.[25] He searches for them and cares for them.[26] He leads them, feeds them, and restores them.[27] He identifies them and judges them.[28] Ezekiel sees Jesus six hundred years before He comes to

20   Ezekiel 17:22-24
21   Revelation 5:12; Matthew 23:12
22   Mark 4:31-32
23   Philippians 2:5-11
24   Ezekiel 21:26-27
25   John 10:12-13
26   John 10:15-16
27   John 10:4, 9
28   John 10:3; Matthew 25:32-33

His sheep and writes down what the Lord God says: 'Woe, shepherds of Israel who have been feeding themselves! Should not the shepherds feed the flock? . . . I will deliver My flock from their mouth . . . Behold, I Myself will search for My sheep and seek them out. As a shepherd cares for his herd in the day when he is among his scattered sheep, so I will care for My sheep and will deliver them . . . I will feed My flock and I will lead them to rest . . . I will seek the lost, bring back the scattered, bind up the broken and strengthen the sick . . . I will deliver My flock, and they will no longer be a prey; and I will judge between one sheep and another.'[29] Jesus is seen in the Scriptures as the Good Shepherd who delivers, feeds, and judges His flock."

"Surely, He is the Shepherd," Jonathan exclaimed.

"Tell us more, Teacher," Cleopas sincerely requested.

"Many times,[30] Ezekiel sees the Son of God, the 'God-Man.' In a pre-incarnate appearance of the Son of God, Ezekiel sees and takes instruction from One Who measures the temple. He was a Man Who appeared in Divine glory.[31] Repeatedly, Ezekiel sees this God-Man, Who is described as 'a likeness as the appearance of a man; from His loins and downward there was the appearance of fire, and from His loins and upward the appearance of brightness, like the appearance of glowing metal.'[32] The God-Man, Jesus, is seen in the Tanakh."

---

29   Ezekiel 34:1-2, 10-12, 15-16, 22
30   Ezekiel 1:26-28; Ezekiel 8:2; Ezekiel 40:3; Ezekiel 43:6; Ezekiel 47:3
31   Ezekiel 40:2-5
32   Ezekiel 8:2

CHAPTER 8

CONVERSING IN HOSEA, JOEL, AMOS

"What about Hosea?" asked Cleopas. "Is he not a type of Christ?"

"What are you seeing, Cleopas?" Jesus asked with a wide smile on His face.

"Oh, I don't know. It's just that Hosea seems like the prototypical selfless redeemer. I mean, Gomer . . . really!" Cleopas said with a real tone of disgust in his voice.

"Sin is disgusting," Jesus asserted. "Gomer represents the sin of mankind. And Hosea represents the love and selflessness that it takes to buy back that which was lost. Hosea stands as a type of Christ—the compassionate Redeemer—when he redeems Gomer from the slave market,[1] even as Christ redeems man from the slavery of sin.[2] Yes, Cleopas, Hosea is a somewhat uncomfortable type of Christ. But then again . . . redemption is, by necessity, uncomfortable!"

Jesus slid over to be a bit closer to Jonathan. "Earlier this morning, what did the women who went to the tomb report to you?"

"They said that our Lord was not there and that He had risen from the dead."

"That's what they said," lamented Cleopas. "But we did not see Him."

---

1   Hosea 1:2; 3:1-2
2   John 8:34-36

With a reassuring look, Jesus responded to Cleopas' doubt. "You know, Cleopas, the prophet Hosea pointed to the resurrection of the Christ[3] and the ensuing resurrection of His followers[4] when He wrote, 'He will revive us after two days; He will raise us up on the third day, that we may live before Him.'[5] Know this, Cleopas, the resurrection of Jesus is seen in the Tanakh."

Jesus suggested that they get back to the road and back to their journey. The three men got up off the ground where they were sitting and made their way back to the road to Emmaus.

"So, Jesus is alive?" Cleopas asked. Some part of him was genuinely asking while a larger part of him, now, was actually proclaiming it as a fact.

"And He is God," Jonathan added as though it was, at least, a logical progression from the idea of Him being raised from the dead.

It was time for Jesus to reinforce the answers. "Yes to both assertions. Jesus is risen, and Jesus is God. And just as Hosea pointed to His resurrection, he also pointed to His divinity. Since Jesus is God, He speaks as God. He says things like, 'I desire compassion and not sacrifice.'[6] When Hosea recounts the words of God—'I delight in loyalty rather than sacrifice'[7]—he is pointing to Jesus' divinity. Jesus is seen in the Scriptures."

Cleopas began to notice how many people were walking in the other direction on the road. "All these people going to Jerusalem almost seem like they are part of a mini exodus." Cleopas tried his hand at comedy.

"If that's the exodus, then where are we going? Egypt?" Jonathan countered Cleopas' attempt at humor.

Jesus chuckled. "Even as God called Israel out of Egypt in the Exodus,[8] so, too, God the Father called Jesus out of Egypt.[9] Hosea, thus, prophesied, 'When

---

3   Luke 24:46
4   Ephesians 2:6
5   Hosea 6:2; 1 Corinthians 15:4
6   Matthew 9:13
7   Hosea 6:6
8   Exodus 12:42
9   Matthew 2:15

Israel was a youth I loved him, and out of Egypt I called My son.'[10] Jesus, the Son, is seen in the Prophets.

"Joel prophesied about the return of Christ and the end of the age[11] as he pictured it as a time of unparalleled tribulation.[12] 'Blow a trumpet in Zion, and sound an alarm on My holy mountain! Let all the inhabitants of the land tremble, for the day of the LORD is coming; surely it is near, a day of darkness and gloom, a day of clouds and thick darkness. As the dawn is spread over the mountains, so there is a great and mighty people; there has never been *anything* like it, nor will there be again after it.'[13] Christ's second coming is seen in the Prophets."

Jesus stopped for a moment and put His hand on His chin as if He were deep in thought. "So, Jonathan, what do you think is going to happen next if Jesus has been resurrected like the women reported to you early this morning?"

Jonathan looked at Cleopas. "I think . . . " Jonathan struggled to continue his prognostication.

Cleopas jumped in and began to swim in the prognostication waters. "Jesus will ascend to the Father, and then He will send the Holy Spirit.[14] He told us clearly that He would send the Spirit."

Jesus nodded. "This is what is going to happen next. The pouring out of the Spirit is both promised by Jesus and prophesied by the prophet Joel. In fact, the Spirit will be poured out fifty days from now. Joel prophesied about this glorious event when he wrote, 'It will come about after this that I will pour out My Spirit on all mankind; and your sons and daughters will prophesy, your old men will dream dreams, your young men will see visions. Even on the male and female servants I will pour out My Spirit in those days.'[15] Jesus is seen in the Tanakh."

---

10   Hosea 11:1
11   Joel 2:30-31
12   Matthew 24:3, 21
13   Joel 2:1-2
14   John 16:7-15; Acts 1:8
15   Joel 2:28-29

Jesus continued. "Joel also prophesied about the Messiah's return and the final judgment in the end times when he referenced God's proclamation, 'I will gather all the nations and bring them down to the valley of Jehoshaphat. Then I will enter into judgment with them there.'[16] God then says, 'Put in the sickle, for the harvest is ripe. Come, tread, for the wine press is full; the vats overflow, for their wickedness is great.'[17] Jesus' disciple, John, will be given a vision of the end times that looks very similar to Joel's prophecy. 'So the angel swung his sickle to the earth and gathered the clusters from the vine of the earth, and threw them into the great wine press of the wrath of God.'[18] These descriptions of the return of Christ and the end times are made eight hundred years apart. Christ is seen in the Tanakh, since 'He was.' He fulfills what is seen in the Tanakh because 'He is." And He will be seen in the later visions because 'He is to come.' Christ is seen in the Scriptures."

Cleopas suggested, "So, Jesus is both Savior and Judge."

"Yes," Jesus agreed. "Amos is a prophet who announces God's judgment. Throughout his prophecies, he speaks forth God's judgment over the nations and over Israel. In so doing, he points to Jesus inasmuch as Jesus is the One Who judges. More specifically, he points to the Trinity. Jesus says, 'But even if I do judge, My judgment is true; for I am not alone in it, but I and the Father who sent Me.'[19] Jesus 'is the One who has been appointed by God as Judge of the living and the dead. Of Him, all the prophets bear witness that through His name, everyone who believes in Him receives forgiveness of sins.'[20] And so, Amos not only points to Jesus the Judge[21] but also to Jesus the Savior and Restorer.[22] 'In that day I will raise up the fallen booth of David,

---

16   Joel 3:2
17   Joel 3:13
18   Revelation 14:19; 19:15
19   John 8:16
20   Acts 10:42-43
21   Amos 1:1-9:10
22   Amos 9:11-15

and wall up its breaches; I will also raise up its ruins and rebuild it as in the days of old.'[23] Jesus is seen in the Prophets."

The three men continued to walk down the road. Storm clouds began to grow in the sky above them, and as they covered the sun, the afternoon daylight began to dim.

Jesus inquired of Jonathan, "Where were you when Jesus was being crucified?"

"I was there. Cleopas was there. Many of us were there."

"What do you remember?"

"As He hung there, dying on the cross, it suddenly became very dark."

"Yes," muttered Cleopas, entering into the conversation. "It was very strange. It was like night during the day."

"And then His last breath," Jonathan reminisced sadly, seeming to look far away toward the hills.

"The earthquake," Cleopas whispered.

Jesus entered in. "These things may have happened only three days ago, but they were first mentioned in the Divine conversation over eight hundred years ago. The prophet Amos saw, in some detail, Christ's last hours as He hung on the cross and darkness fell over the whole land at noon,[24] and then the earth shook.[25] Amos prophesied, 'It will come about in that day . . . that I will make the sun go down at noon and make the earth dark in broad daylight'[26] and because of this will not the land quake.'[27] Details of Jesus' crucifixion are seen in the Tanakh."

---

23   Amos 9:11
24   Mark 15:33
25   Matthew 27:51
26   Amos 8:9
27   Amos 8:8

CHAPTER 9

CONVERSING IN OBADIAH, JONAH, MICAH, NAHUM

"So you saw Him die on the cross but you still, as yet, have seen Him risen from the dead?" Jesus inquired of Jonathan.

Jonathan answered immediately. "We know He has died. We saw it. We do not know if He has risen. We have not seen it."

Jesus stopped on the road. He turned His face up to the heavens and raised His hands. "He has risen. He has risen, indeed."

Jonathan and Cleopas stared at each other, half-alarmed and half euphoric.

"Do you remember how the prophet Joel described the Messiah as both Savior and Judge?" Jesus prompted. "The prophet Obadiah also points to Him Who has been raised from the dead as Judge. 'Therefore having overlooked the times of ignorance, God is now declaring to men that all people everywhere should repent because He has fixed a day in which He will judge the world in righteousness through a Man Whom He has appointed, having furnished proof to all men by raising Him from the dead.'[1] Obadiah writes, 'For the day of the Lord draws near on all the nations. As you have done, it will be done to you. Your dealings will return on your own head. Because just as you drank on My holy mountain, all the nations will drink continually. They will drink and swallow and become as if they had never existed.'[2] Jesus the Judge is seen in the Scriptures."

---

1   Acts 17:30-31
2   Obadiah 15-16

Jesus continued. "Like Joel, Obadiah also points to Christ the Savior[3] when he prophesies how in the midst of Divine judgement there will be those who escape and are restored. He writes, 'But on Mount Zion there will be those who escape, and it will be holy. And the house of Jacob will possess their possessions.'[4] The Prophets show forth Jesus as both Judge and Savior."

The three men walked on in silence for a few minutes. Jonathan was clearly lost in thought.

Jesus broke the silence. "What are you pondering, Jonathan?"

"We talked about those last hours when Jesus lay dying on the cross; the darkness and the earthquake. I keep seeing in my mind that inscription above His head: 'This is the king of the Jews.'[5] Is He the king of the Jews?"

"He is[6]; yet, He is much more. His kingdom, which He often spoke of, is not of this earth.[7] His is the kingdom of God. He is King over all. The prophet Obadiah points to Jesus the Possessor of the kingdom[8] when he proclaims, 'And the kingdom will be the Lord's.'[9] Jesus the King is seen in the Scriptures."

Jesus stopped and bent over, and as had become His custom, He began to draw in the dirt. "What does it look like to you, Jonathan?"

"It looks like a big fish that lives in the sea."

"What does that make you think of?"

"Jonah, of course."

"Yes. And also Jesus, as Jonah is a type of Jesus. Three days and three nights in the belly of a whale[10] foreshadows three days and three nights in the grave.[11] Just as an ominous situation for Jonah led to salvation for many,[12] so, too, an

---

3   Luke 2:11
4   Obadiah 17
5   Luke 23:38
6   Luke 23:3
7   Matthew 16:28; Mark 14:25; Luke 11:20; John 18:36
8   John 18:36
9   Obadiah 21
10 Jonah 1:17
11 Matthew 12:40
12 Jonah 3:5-10

ominous situation for Jesus led to salvation for all.[13] Jonah's salvation story pales in comparison to Jesus' salvation story. Jesus would say, in comparing Himself to Jonah, 'something greater than Jonah is here.'[14] Jesus is seen in the Scriptures in Jonah's experience that is then amplified in Jesus' own experience. Jonah's experience prefigures the death, burial, and resurrection of Jesus Christ.[15]

"Christ is seen often in the Prophets," Jesus concluded. "Micah, for example, pictures the Messiah, saying, 'I will put them together like sheep in the fold; like a flock in the midst of its pasture . . . they break out, pass through the gate and go out by it. So their king goes on before them, and the Lord at their head.'[16] Over seven hundred years later, Jesus said, 'Truly, truly, I say to you, I am the door of the sheep . . . I am the door; if anyone enters through Me, he will be saved, and will go in and out and find pasture.'[17] He also said, 'I am the Good Shepherd'[18] who 'when he puts forth all his own, he goes ahead of them, and the sheep follow him because they know his voice.'[19] Jesus, the Good Shepherd, is once again seen in the Scriptures."

Just then, a funeral procession passed by them as they were walking on the road. Many people were weeping and wailing. "Do you see the fruit of the corruption of this world," Jesus probed. "It will not always be this way.

"A day is coming when the righteous reign of Christ over the whole world will be established. When He returns, He Himself will be the lamp that illumines the new Jerusalem[20] and 'the nations will walk by its light, and the kings of the earth will bring their glory into it.'[21] Death will be no more,[22] and peace will reign in its place.[23]

---

13   John 3:16
14   Matthew 12:41
15   Matthew 12:39-41
16   Micah 2:12-13
17   John 10:7-9
18   John 10:11
19   John 10:4
20   Rev 21:23
21   Revelation 21:24
22   Revelation 21:4
23   Revelation 20:2

"The prophet Micah portrays this incredible scene when he writes, 'And it will come about in the last days that the mountain of the house of the Lord will be established as the chief of the mountains. It will be raised above the hills, and the peoples will stream to it . . . for from Zion will go forth the law, even the word of the Lord from Jerusalem. And He will judge between many peoples and render decisions for mighty, distant nations. Then they will hammer their swords into plowshares and their spears into pruning hooks; nation will not lift up sword against nation, and never again will they train for war. Each of them will sit under his vine and under his fig tree, with no one to make them afraid, for the mouth of the Lord of hosts has spoken . . . we will walk in the name of the Lord our God forever and ever.'[24] Jesus will reign in the new heavens and the new earth where there will be peace, no fear, and no death forevermore. Both Jesus and this picture of Heaven are seen in the Scriptures."

"Teacher," Jonathan asked, "may I ask you a question?"

"Yes."

"Why was the Messiah not born in Jerusalem?"

"Jesus was born in Bethlehem, an unlikely but prophesied place for His birth. Over seven hundred years before the Messiah was born in Bethlehem,[25] Micah prophesied concerning Bethlehem, 'From you One will go forth for Me to be ruler in Israel.'[26] The prophet also writes that the Messiah will come 'when she who is in labor has borne a child.'[27] He 'will arise and shepherd the flock.'[28] He 'will be great to the ends of the earth. And this One will be our peace.'[29] Moreover, 'His goings forth are from long ago, from the days of eternity.'"[30]

Jonathan, almost interrupting Jesus, cried out with a loud voice, "This is incredible. This is truly amazing. How can this be? How can the Christ be

---

24   Micah 4:1-5
25   Matthew 2:8-11
26   Micah 5:2
27   Micah 5:3
28   Micah 5:4
29   Micah 5:4-5
30   Micah 5:2

so clearly pictured by one who prophesied so many years ago? Indeed, Jesus fulfills every single one of these specific prophecies.[31] This is nothing less than seeing in the Scriptures with our own eyes the Son of God, the Christ—Jesus Himself."

"Now I have a question, Teacher," declared Cleopas. "When we were in Gethsemane with Jesus the night before His crucifixion and the crowd came to arrest Him, one of our own drew out his sword. Jesus told him to put his sword away.[32] Yet, Jesus told us previously that He actually came to earth to bring a sword.[33] How can He tell us to put away our swords and at the same time say that He has come to bring a sword?"

"Jesus does not ask His disciples to fight or to kill others. Thus, He instructs you to put your sword away. However, He does warn you that because of Him, others will want to kill you. Thus, He says that He came to bring a sword. Your sword is not to come against others, but their swords will come against you. Jesus even said that a man's enemies would be the members of his own household.[34] Micah saw this long ago and wrote, 'For son treats father contemptuously, daughter rises up against her mother, daughter-in-law against her mother-in-law; a man's enemies are the men of his own household.'[35] Jesus is seen in the Prophets."

A storm was quickly approaching. "Look," Jonathan pointed ahead. "There is a roadside market. Perhaps, there, we can take cover from the storm."

The three men ran ahead. Arriving at the market, they found a place to sit under the canopy of one of the stalls. Suddenly, a big roar of thunder echoed through the market. At the same time, a bolt of lightning seemed to strike just on the other side of the road where they had just been walking.

"Wow, that was really close," Cleopas said with a little shake in his voice.

"Who controls the storms?" Jesus asked.

---

31   Luke 2:7; John 10:11; Revelation 11:4; Ephesians 2:14; John 1:1, 14
32   Matthew 26:47, 51-52
33   Matthew 10:34
34   Matthew 10:35-36
35   Micah 7:6

"Well, God, of course," Jonathan said decisively.

Jesus was quick to confirm his answer. "Indeed, all things were created by, for, and through the Son of God Who is the Sustainer and Controller of all creation.[36] The prophet Nahum points to Him, Who controls the winds, storms, and clouds as well as the land, trees, seas, rivers, mountains, and the earth and all its inhabitants.[37] The Son of God is seen in the Scriptures."

---

36 Colossians 1:16-17
37 Nahum 1:3-5

CHAPTER 10

CONVERSING IN HABAKKUK, ZEPHANIAH, HAGGAI

As the storm continued to throw down lightning bolts from the sky, Cleopas, always one to try to lighten the mood in the midst of tension, half-joked, "So the Son of God saves me from my sins and from this storm."

Jesus chuckled just a bit. "Yes, Cleopas, and the prophet Habakkuk highlights the Son of God as the Savior. He repeatedly refers to God in the context of His provision for salvation. It is God Who saves. As you know, the name 'Jesus' is the name 'God saves.' Jesus is God, and Jesus is the God Who saves. So, whether it is God Who rides on His 'chariots of salvation'[1] or God Who goes forth for the salvation of His anointed people,[2] it is literally 'God saves,' or 'Jesus,' Who is ultimately being referenced by the prophet. So, when Habakkuk proclaims, 'Yet I will exult in the Lord, I will rejoice in the God of my salvation,'[3] he is seeing Jesus. Jesus is seen in the Tanakh."

"So, as we have said, Jesus is Savior, but He is also Judge," Jonathan pondered. "It seems as though His actions as Judge will especially be seen in the context of His second coming."

"The judgment of God is a terrible thing to see," added Cleopas. "God have mercy!"

---

1   Habakkuk 3:8
2   Habakkuk 3:13
3   Habakkuk 3:18

"He does," Jesus confirmed. "However, His judgment when He returns is very real. The prophet Zephaniah paints such a picture. He prophesies concerning the second coming of Christ. He proclaims the word of the Lord, Who says, 'I will remove man and beast; I will remove the birds of the sky and the fish of the sea, and the ruins along with the wicked; and I will cut off man from the face of the earth.'[4] Jesus described it this way: 'The Son of Man will send forth His angels, and they will gather out of His kingdom all stumbling blocks, and those who commit lawlessness and will throw them into the furnace of fire.'"[5]

"Again, Zephaniah points to the second coming of Christ when he writes, 'A day of wrath is that day, a day of trouble and distress, a day of destruction and desolation, a day of darkness and gloom, a day of clouds and thick darkness.'[6] Jesus refers to this day saying, 'But immediately after the tribulation of those days, the sun will be darkened, and the moon will not give its light, and the stars will fall from the sky, and the powers of the heavens will be shaken.'"[7]

Zephaniah alludes to the second coming of Christ as he references seven times the 'day of the Lord.'[8] In the end times, two very different groups will be gathered together: those who have been purchased as firstfruits to God in whom 'no lie was found in their mouth; they are blameless,'[9] and the nations that will be judged when 'from His mouth comes a sharp sword, so that with it He may strike down the nations, and He will rule them with a rod of iron; and He treads the wine press of the fierce wrath of God, the Almighty.'[10]

"Zephaniah sees the Christ in the gathering together of both of these groups. First, he writes, 'The remnant of Israel will do no wrong and tell no

---

4　Zephaniah 1:3
5　Matthew 13:41-42
6　Zephaniah 1:15
7　Matthew 24:29
8　Zephaniah 1:7-8, 14, 18; 2:2-3
9　Revelation 14:5
10　Revelation 19:15

lies.'[11] He also writes, 'Indeed, My decision is to gather nations, to assemble kingdoms, to pour out on them My indignation, all My burning anger; for all the earth will be devoured by the fire of My zeal.'[12] Jesus, His second coming, and His activities in His second coming are seen in the Scriptures."

The storm ended. "Let us commence with our journey," suggested Cleopas.

"And perhaps the Teacher will commence with His teachings," requested Jonathan.

"Let's consider the temple again," Jesus proposed. "The second temple was completed some five hundred years before the coming of Christ. Ten years or so before His coming, Herod the Great completely overhauled the second temple and built it into a much grander structure. Around the time of the building of the second temple, the prophet Haggai wrote down God's words, 'I will fill this house with glory . . . the latter glory of this house will be greater than the former . . . and in this place I will give peace.'[13] Jesus, the greater Temple,[14] fulfills God's promise to 'fill this house with glory,'[15] to make the 'latter glory of this house . . . greater than the former,'[16] and to 'in this place . . . give peace.'[17] In Haggai's prophecy concerning the temple, Jesus is seen in the Scriptures."

"Cleopas," asked Jesus. "What do you know of Jesus' genealogy?"

"His legal genealogy is traced through Joseph, while His biological genealogy is traced through Mary."

Jesus continued. "The coming of the Messiah is seen in a prophecy given by Haggai concerning Zerubbabel. 'I will take you, Zerubbabel, son of Shealtiel, My servant . . . and I will make you like a signet ring, for I have chosen you.'[18] Zerubbabel is a signet ring, one who seals together both

---

11   Zephaniah 3:13
12   Zephaniah 3:8
13   Haggai 2:7-9
14   Matthew 12:6; 26:61
15   Luke 22:53
16   Luke 2:27-32
17   Luke 2:14
18   Haggai 2:23

branches of the lineage of Christ; that is, the line of Joseph[19] coming through Zerubbabel, coming through Solomon, coming through David,[20] as well as the line of Mary[21] coming through Zerubbabel, coming through Nathan, coming through David. And so, through Zerubbabel as a signet ring, Christ is seen in the Scriptures."

19   Matthew 1:12
20   Psalm 132:11
21   Luke 3:27

CHAPTER 11

CONVERSING IN ZECHARIAH, MALACHI

"Jonathan, do you remember our conversations about the 'angel of the Lord'? Jesus asked, expecting a positive response.

"Yes," Jonathan responded. "The 'angel of the Lord' appears in the Scriptures as the Son of God."

Cleopas eagerly added, "He is God Who can be seen."[1]

"Yes," Jesus agreed. "The prophet Zechariah writes about Him—the angel of the Lord—in the context of the salvation of Joshua the high priest from Satan's accusations and then describes that salvation in terms of the need to put on clothes that 'the angel' provides."

Jesus explained further, "The prophet Zechariah recalled,[2] 'Then he showed me Joshua the high priest standing before the angel of the Lord, and Satan standing at his right hand to accuse him. Now Joshua was clothed with filthy garments and standing before the angel.' Then the angel of the Lord said, 'Remove the filthy garments from him . . . see, I have taken your iniquity away from you and will clothe you with festal robes.' Then Zechariah said, 'Let them put a clean turban on his head.' So they put a clean turban on his head and clothed him with festal robes while the angel of the Lord was standing by."

---

1   John 1:1, 14, 18
2   Zechariah 3:1-5

"Wait," urged Cleopas. "I remember a parable Jesus told us in which salvation depended on wearing the right clothes."

Jesus expanded on what Cleopas had remembered. "Christ told a parable to the Pharisees that concluded with the pronouncement concerning the requirement to have on only the clothes that were provided in order to get into the wedding feast—accepting God's provision for forgiveness in order to be saved.[3] Salvation must come from Christ, 'the Angel of the Lord,' and His provision. This truth about Christ and salvation is seen in the Tanakh."

The wind from the storm had blown some branches off the trees that stood just off the side of the road. Jonathan picked up a branch. He held it up in front of Jesus and smiled. His expression somehow said, "Another marker that points to the Messiah."

Taking the branch from Jonathan, Jesus acknowledged what was being said. "The prophet Zechariah prophesied concerning the coming Messiah, calling Him, 'My servant the Branch.[4] He also makes mention of this Branch when he explains how the Messiah will be both King and Priest: 'Behold, a man whose name is Branch, for He will branch out from where He is; and He will build the temple of the Lord. It is He who will build the temple of the Lord, and He who will bear the honor and sit and rule on His throne. Thus, He will be a priest on His throne, and the counsel of peace will be between the two offices.'[5] Jesus, who is the Branch and the Temple,[6] is seen in the Scriptures."

Jesus broke the branch in half. He put the one part across the other part in order to form a cross. "This," he said emphatically, "is ultimately how the Branch must serve."

"Zechariah paints a picture of the Messiah and His perfect work on the cross. He prophesies, 'For behold, the stone that I have set before Joshua; on one stone are seven eyes. Behold, I will engrave an inscription on it . . .

---

3   Matthew 22:11-14
4   Zechariah 3:8
5   Zechariah 6:12-13
6   Revelation 5:5; Matthew 24:32-33; John 2:19-21; Revelation 21:22

and I will remove the iniquity of that land in one day. In that day . . . every one of you will invite his neighbor to sit under his vine and under his fig tree.'[7] The stone is Christ.[8] The seven eyes depict the perfect vision of God— Jehovah Jireh, 'the God who sees'—regarding man's need[9]; that is, his need for salvation. Messiah would remove iniquity in one monumental day—Friday— when He was crucified and the inscription of the charge against Him read, 'THE KING OF THE JEWS.'[10] Along with renewed relationship between God and man, one of the great results of that monumental day is the renewed fellowship between men accomplished in the ultimate atonement. Christ and His death on a cross are seen in the Scriptures."

A small caravan of pilgrims on their way to Jerusalem passed them by on the other side of the road. A donkey pulled a large cart full of supplies.

"Wow," Cleopas commented, "the weight of the load that the donkey is able to pull is quite impressive."

"True," agreed Jonathan while obviously prepping to say something else. "But just think, brother, how impressive the load that was carried by the donkey one week ago when Jesus entered Jerusalem. That donkey was carrying a Divine load that was full of justice and salvation."

"What you say is true, Jonathan," Jesus concurred. "Moreover, that memorable ride on a donkey that you witnessed one week ago was witnessed by the prophet Zechariah over five hundred years ago. Zechariah prophesied of the Messiah's triumphal entry into Jerusalem[11] as the humble King. 'Rejoice greatly, O daughter of Zion! Shout *in triumph*, O daughter of Jerusalem! Behold, your king is coming to you; He is just and endowed with salvation, humble, and mounted on a donkey, even on a colt, the foal of a donkey.'[12] Even down to the detail of the riding of a donkey, the Messiah is seen in the Tanakh."

---

7   Zechariah 3:9-10
8   1 Corinthians 10:4; Matthew 21:42; Ephesians 2:20
9   Genesis 22:14
10 Mark 15:26
11 Matthew 21:5
12 Zechariah 9:9

"Those in that caravan are on their way to Jerusalem," Cleopas reflected. "We are on our way to Emmaus. Oh, that we, instead, were on our way to the new Jerusalem."

"What a glorious desire." Jonathan put his arm around Cleopas as they continued to walk. "There is no more pain there . . . and no more death."

"Exactly," Cleopas affirmed. "And the nations will enjoy perfect peace as they are ruled by the Lamb of God.[13] What a beautiful picture!"

"It is a marvelous picture," Jesus contributed. "Christ will return, and there will be a new Jerusalem. In fact, Christ's second coming is pictured when Zechariah writes, 'I will cut off the chariot from Ephraim and the horse from Jerusalem; and the bow of war will be cut off. And He will speak peace to the nations; and His dominion will be from sea to sea, and from the River to the ends of the earth.'[14] Christ, the Lamb of God, is seen in the Scriptures."

"Zechariah is a lot like Isaiah," Cleopas concluded.

"In what sense?" questioned Jonathan.

"In that they both see Christ quite often." Cleopas looked at Jesus with an inviting expression.

"Let me respond to your invitation, Cleopas." Jesus chuckled. "Zechariah does see Christ in a variety of ways. He calls Him the Cornerstone, the Tent Peg, and the Bow of battle.[15] Jesus is the Cornerstone.[16] He is the Tent Peg, that on which everything else hangs.[17] He is the Bow of battle.[18] Jesus is seen in the Tanakh."

"This is, certainly, marvelous in our sight," exclaimed Cleopas. "God shows His prophets very specific things over five hundred years before they happen."

Jesus nodded. "Thirty," He whispered.

Jonathan stepped in front of Him. "Thirty what?"

---

13   Revelation 21:3-4, 24; 22:1-5
14   Zechariah 9:10
15   Zechariah 10:4
16   Luke 20:17; Ephesians 2:20; 1 Peter 2:6
17   Isaiah 22:23
18   Jeremiah 51:20

"Zechariah prophesied of Jesus' betrayal by Judas as he wrote of the thirty pieces of silver, which was the price set on Jesus' head that was then used to buy the potter's field which will forevermore be called 'the field of blood.'"[19]

"Teacher, how is the prophecy written?" Cleopas requested.

Jesus again nodded. "It is written, 'If it is good in your sight, give me my wages; but if not, never mind! So they weighed out thirty shekels of silver as my wages.' Then the Lord said, '*Throw it to the potter, that magnificent price at which I was valued by them.*' So, he took the thirty shekels of silver and threw them to the potter in the house of the Lord."[20]

"Even to the smallest of details," Jesus concluded. "Christ is seen in the Prophets. Moreover, He is confirmed as being God. Zechariah's prophecy equates 'the Angel of the Lord' with God Himself: '. . . and the house of David will be like God, like the angel of the Lord before them.'[21] This, of course, is consistent with how 'the angel of the Lord' is presented in many places in the Scriptures, as a Divine being who can be seen by man. This is none other than Jesus Himself in a pre-incarnate appearance in the Scriptures."

"Seeing such details over five hundred years before they occur is impressive," Cleopas remarked as he stared at Jonathan. "We saw details that we did not want to see—Jesus hanging on that cross and the soldiers thrusting that spear into His side." Cleopas hesitated. "No, we did not want to see that."

Jonathan waited for a few seconds and then added, "Some pictures you don't want painted even if the painting is priceless."

Jesus began to teach again. "Zechariah sees a specific scene from the crucifixion of Jesus. 'I will pour out on the house of David and on the inhabitants of Jerusalem, the Spirit of grace and of supplication, so that they will look on Me whom they have pierced; and they will mourn for Him, as one mourns for an only son, and they will weep bitterly over Him like the bitter weeping over

---

19   Matthew 27:8-10
20   Zechariah 11:12-13
21   Zechariah 12:8

a firstborn.'[22] Jesus, the only Son,[23] the firstborn,[24] would be pierced in the side[25] and mourned.[26] Jesus and His crucifixion is clearly seen in the Tanakh."

Jesus continued to teach. "Zechariah prophesies, 'In that day a fountain will be opened for the house of David and for the inhabitants of Jerusalem, for sin and for impurity.'[27] Jesus is that cleansing fountain.[28] His blood will take away all sin and impurity.[29] As is often done in a variety of ways, God's plan of salvation is pictured in the Scriptures. 'God saves' shows up in the Tanakh. Jesus is seen over five hundred years ago in the Prophets."

"Where did the disciples go after their Shepherd was arrested in Gethsemane?" Jesus abruptly posed the question as He began to slowly walk backwards away from Jonathan and Cleopas.

The two men quickly scampered back and grabbed hold of Jesus. "Teacher," bemoaned Jonathan, "continue to walk with us to Emmaus."

Jesus began to walk forward again. "Where did the sheep go when the Shepherd was struck down? Did He not say to them, 'You will all fall away because of Me this night'?"[30]

"Yes, He did say it," Jonathan answered reluctantly.

"And, yes, we did fall away," responded Cleopas even more reluctantly.

Jesus looked down at the ground. "The prophet Zechariah wrote, 'Awake, O sword, against My Shepherd, and against the man, My Associate . . . Strike the Shepherd that the sheep may be scattered.'[31] The betrayal of Jesus is seen in the Tanakh."

Jesus now looked up to the heavens. He smiled. "Zechariah is a prophet. He is a seer. He is, one might say, a painter. Zechariah paints a vivid picture

---

22 Zechariah 12:10
23 John 3:16
24 Romans 8:29
25 John 19:34
26 Revelation 1:7
27 Zechariah 13:1
28 1 John 1:9; John 4:14
29 John 1:29
30 Matthew 26:31; John 16:32
31 Zechariah 13:7

of the end times including the final siege of Jerusalem, the second coming of the Messiah, and a picture of His kingdom, the new heavens and the new earth.

"Listen to the Word of God." Jesus began to recite: 'Behold, a day is coming for the Lord when the spoil taken from you will be divided among you. For I will gather all the nations against Jerusalem to battle, and the city will be captured, the houses plundered, the women ravished and half of the city exiled, but the rest of the people will not be cut off from the city. Then the Lord will go forth and fight against those nations, as when He fights on a day of battle. In that day His feet will stand on the Mount of Olives, which is in front of Jerusalem on the east; and the Mount of Olives will be split in its middle from east to west by a very large valley, so that half of the mountain will move toward the north and the other half toward the south. You will flee by the valley of My mountains, for the valley of the mountains will reach to Azel; yes, you will flee just as you fled before the earthquake in the days of Uzziah king of Judah. Then the Lord, my God, will come, and all the holy ones with Him! In that day there will be no light; the luminaries will dwindle. For it will be a unique day which is known to the Lord, neither day nor night, but it will come about that at evening time there will be light. And in that day living waters will flow out of Jerusalem, half of them toward the eastern sea and the other half toward the western sea; it will be in summer as well as in winter. And the Lord will be king over all the earth; in that day the Lord will be the only one, and His name the only one. All the land will be changed into a plain from Geba to Rimmon south of Jerusalem; but Jerusalem will rise and remain on its site from Benjamin's Gate as far as the place of the First Gate to the Corner Gate, and from the Tower of Hananel to the king's wine presses. People will live in it, and there will no longer be a curse, for Jerusalem will dwell in security. Now this will be the plague with which the Lord will strike all the peoples who have gone to war against Jerusalem; their flesh will rot while they stand on their feet, and their eyes will rot in their sockets, and their tongue will rot in their mouth. It will come about in that day that a great panic from the Lord will fall on them; and they will seize one another's hand, and the hand of one will be lifted against the hand of another. Judah also will fight at Jerusalem; and the wealth of all the surrounding nations will be gathered, gold and silver and garments in great abundance. So also like this plague will be the plague on the horse, the mule, the camel, the donkey and all the cattle that will be in those camps. Then it will come about that any who are left of all the nations that went against Jerusalem will go up from year to year to worship the King, the Lord of hosts.'"[32]

Jesus, again, looked up to the heavens. He lifted His arms. "God be glorified, for He has shown Himself. He has shown Himself in the Prophets and in all the Tanakh."

As Jesus, Cleopas, and Jonathan continued to walk down the road together, they passed two men who were arguing with each other. One of the men was, obviously, very disgruntled and kept yelling, "I want justice."

Jesus used the situation to begin His teaching again. "In the context of the people demanding, 'Where is the God of Justice?,'[33] Malachi paints a picture of the second coming of the Lord, Who will someday arrive as the God of justice. 'But who can endure the day of His coming? And who can stand when He appears? For He is like a refiner's fire and like fullers' soap. He will sit as a smelter and purifier of silver, and He will purify the sons of Levi and refine them like gold and silver, so that they may present to the Lord offerings in righteousness. Then the offering of Judah and Jerusalem will be pleasing to the Lord as in the days of old and as in former years. Then I will draw near to you for judgment.'"[34]

"At that time, a book will be opened to distinguish between the righteous and the wicked,[35] and the righteous will join the God of justice[36] in His fiery

---

32 Zephaniah 14:1-16
33 Malachi 2:17
34 Malachi 3:2-5
35 Revelation 20:12
36 Revelation 17:14; Revelation 19:11-16

judgment against the wicked.[37] Malachi pictures this and writes, 'A book of remembrance was written before Him for those who fear the Lord and who esteem His name.' The Lord then says, 'They will be Mine, on the day that I prepare My own possession, and I will spare them as a man spares his own son who serves him. So you will again distinguish between the righteous and the wicked, between one who serves God and one who does not serve Him. For behold, the day is coming, burning like a furnace; and all the arrogant and every evildoer will be chaff; and the day that is coming will set them ablaze . . . so that it will leave them neither root nor branch. But for you who fear My name, the sun of righteousness will rise with healing in its wings; and you will go forth and skip about like calves from the stall. You will tread down the wicked, for they will be ashes under the soles of your feet on the day which I am preparing.'[38] Hence, Christ and the events surrounding His second coming are seen in the Scriptures.

"If there is a second coming then, of course, there is a first coming." Jesus was fishing for something. "Christ does come initially as the 'God of justice' but in a different way from how He comes as the 'God of justice' when He returns.

"Malachi points to the incarnation of God as he responds to the people's question, 'Where's the God of justice?' Of course, God's justice is most profoundly found in His coming in the form of Jesus Christ.[39] Hence, Malachi writes, 'Behold, I am going to send My messenger, and he will clear the way before Me. And the Lord, whom you seek, will suddenly come to His temple; and the messenger of the covenant, in whom you delight, behold, He is coming.'[40] This, of course, is a picture of the coming of Jesus Christ, the Lord God. Paradoxically—as the Trinity remains a paradox—what we see here is God sending God, and thus, God becoming a Man.[41] Mercifully, this

---

37 Revelation 20:14-15
38 Malachi 3:16-4:3
39 John 3:19
40 Malachi 3:1
41 John 1:1, 14

God of justice will come as Savior and not yet as Judge.[42] The God of justice comes 'like a refiner's fire and like fuller's soap.'[43] Herein, we see the mercy of God. A refiner does not destroy. He purifies; he burns away everything that is not pure.[44] A fuller's soap is the soap that can clean even the worst stain. It is what makes clothes white again. God the Savior is pictured as a 'smelter and purifier,' Who 'purifies' and 'refines' His people so that they can be right with Him again and 'so that they may present to the Lord offerings in righteousness.'[45] God the Savior is pictured as One who sits as a Refiner and a Fuller as He works on His people showing the patience and concern that He has for His people. And so, in a variety of ways, the prophet Malachi paints a clear picture of the incarnation of God in Jesus Christ."

Just then, a commotion began to be heard as a large crowd seemed to be gathering some distance down the road.

Cleopas squinted to try to see what was going on. "Someone is riding a horse." He turned his ear toward the commotion. "People are yelling something about Rome."

Jonathan, whose eyesight and hearing were considerably better than Cleopas', saw and heard what was going on. "It is a Roman authority. People are paying their respects to him, crying out in loud voices, 'Great is Rome.' Some soldiers are clearing the crowds and yelling, 'Make way for the authority of Rome.'"

"How ridiculous!" murmured Cleopas with a hint of anger and disgust.

"Do not be angry, my friend." Jesus patted Cleopas on the back. "There is One Who holds all authority Who rightly had one going before Him to prepare His way. The coming of the Messiah was announced by a messenger who prepared the way before Him[46] by preaching repentance to 'turn the hearts of the fathers back to the children.'[47]

---

42   John 3:17
43   Malachi 3:2
44   Matthew 3:11-12; 1 Peter 4:12-13; 1 Corinthians 3:13
45   Malachi 3:3
46   Mark 1:4-8
47   Luke 1:17; Malachi 3:7; 4:6

Malachi envisioned this and wrote, 'Behold, I am going to send My messenger, and he will clear the way before Me.'[48] This messenger, of course, is John the Baptist,[49] and the One He is announcing is Jesus Christ, the Son of God.[50] In this way, Jesus Christ, the Son of God, the Messiah, is seen in the Prophets, the Scriptures, the Tanakh."

---

48 Malachi 3:1
49 Matthew 3:1-3
50 Mark 1:1-3

KETUVIM
CONVERSATIONS
(THE WRITINGS)

CHAPTER 12

CONVERSING IN PSALMS

Jesus drew on the ground, '1' and '2.' "The '1' is the Law. We have seen Christ in the Law. The '2' is the Prophets. We have seen Christ in the Prophets. What is '3'?"

Jonathan and Cleopas answered together, "It is the Writings. Show us Christ in the Writings," they both pleaded.

"Christ is seen in all of the Tanakh." Jesus wiped away the numbers that He had drawn in the dirt. "The psalmist writes of the kings and rulers—the Romans and the Jews—who came against Jesus to condemn Him. 'The kings of the earth take their stand and the rulers take counsel together against the Lord and against His Anointed.'"[1]

"It happened just as the psalmist said," Jonathan proclaimed with a sense of wonder. "Indeed, 'all the chief priests and the elders of the people conferred together against Jesus to put Him to death; and they bound Him, and led Him away and delivered Him to Pilate the governor.'"[2]

Jesus bent down again and wrote in the dirt, '3.' "Surely, the Messiah is seen in the Writings.

"When Jesus came up out of the waters of baptism, the voice of the Father said, 'This is My beloved Son, in whom I am well-pleased.'[3] The psalmist prefigures this event when he references the Father's declaration, 'You are My Son, today I have begotten You.'[4] Indeed, the begotten Son of God is seen in the Scriptures."

---

1   Psalm 2:2
2   Matthew 27:1-2
3   Matthew 3:17
4   Psalm 2:7; John 3:16

Cleopas stubbed his foot on a root that was sticking up out of the road. He stumbled but caught himself before falling down.

"If you are not careful, you can certainly stumble," Jesus remarked while still looking straight ahead. "While He was still with you, did He not say, 'Blessed is he who keeps from stumbling over Me'?[5] The psalmist puts forth a warning concerning the Son, 'Now therefore, O kings, show discernment; take warning, O judges of the earth. Worship the Lord with reverence and rejoice with trembling. Do homage to the Son, that He not become angry, and you perish in the way, for His wrath may soon be kindled. How blessed are all who take refuge in Him!'[6] In the context of this warning, God the Father references God the Son as 'His Anointed,' 'My King,' 'My Son,' and 'the Son.'[7] Jesus, and even the Trinity, are seen in the Tanakh."

Jesus continued. "God the Father subjects all things to God the Son 'for in subjecting all things to Him, He left nothing that is not subject to Him.'[8] The psalmist writes of God the Father's exaltation of the Son of God. 'Yet You have made him a little lower than the angels, and You crown him with glory and majesty! You make him to rule over the works of Your hands; You have put all things under his feet.'[9] The Son of God is seen in the Scriptures.

"It is the Son of God who will judge the world because the Father 'has fixed a day in which He will judge the world in righteousness through a Man whom He has appointed, having furnished proof to all men by raising Him from the dead.'[10] The psalmist points to the Son of God as Judge when he says, 'But the Lord abides forever; He has established His throne for judgment, and He will judge the world in righteousness; He will execute judgment for the peoples with equity.'[11] The Son of God, the Lord, is seen in the Scriptures.

5   Luke 7:23
6   Psalm 2:10-12
7   Psalm 2:2, 6, 7, 12
8   Hebrews 2:8
9   Psalm 8:5-6
10   Acts 17:31
11   Psalm 9:7-8

"The yet-to-be recognized, risen Christ asked the two men, "Is it true that you have yet to see the risen Christ?"

Looking directly into the eyes of Jesus, Cleopas answered, "It is true. We have not seen Him."

Jonathan hesitated, almost as though he was studying Jesus' face. "Sometimes I feel like I have seen Him. Maybe it's because of how badly I want to see Him. If He is risen, well, that changes everything. Of course, if He is not risen, then we are of all men most to be pitied."

Jesus put His arm around Jonathan. In a reassuring voice, He declared, "The psalmist points to the fact that it would be impossible for the Son of God to be held by the power of death.[12] He writes about One who sounds like the Son of God in that He talks about the joy He has over His people who are on the earth and about the joy of being seated at the right hand of God the Father.[13] He says, 'As for the saints who are in the earth, they are the majestic ones in whom is all my delight.'[14] Then the Son says to the Father, 'You will not abandon my soul to Sheol; nor will You allow Your Holy One to undergo decay. You will make known to me the path of life; in Your presence is fullness of joy; in Your right hand there are pleasures forever.'[15] The resurrection and ascension of the Christ are seen in the Scriptures."[16]

"Look at that large rock that is at the bottom of this hill." Jesus pointed in the appropriate direction. "What is so majestic about a rock?"

Jonathan placed his hand on his chin. "A rock is sturdy. It is steady. It is immovable. It is steadfast. It is durable."

"It is dependable," added Cleopas.

"Yes, it is dependable," confirmed Jesus. "The prophets often allude to the coming Messiah in the context of Him being described as the Rock Who is the Horn of salvation. David says, 'The Lord is my rock and my fortress and

---

12   Acts 2:24
13   Hebrews 12:2
14   Psalm 16:3
15   Psalm 16:10-11
16   Mark 16:6-7, 19

my deliverer; my God, my rock, in whom I take refuge, my shield and the horn of my salvation, my stronghold and my refuge; my savior, You save me from violence.'[17] The Messiah has been raised up as that Horn of salvation,[18] Who is the Rock[19] and Who comes from the house of David.[20]

"The psalmist repeatedly describes the Messiah as the Rock and Savior in his song of thanksgiving for God's deliverance: 'The Lord is my rock and my fortress and my deliverer, my God, my rock, in whom I take refuge; my shield and the horn of my salvation, my stronghold. I call upon the Lord, who is worthy to be praised, and I am saved from my enemies.'[21] The psalmist continues, 'For who is God, but the Lord? And who is a rock, except our God.'[22] In addition, he writes, 'You have also given me the shield of Your salvation.'[23] The psalmist then sums up the main theme of his song by saying, 'The Lord lives, and blessed be my rock; and exalted be the God of my salvation.'[24] So, too, another Psalm is concluded with the cry, 'O Lord, my rock and my Redeemer.'[25] The Son of God, the Rock and Savior, is seen in the Writings.

"How can God be with Himself?" Jesus asked with a furrowed brow. 'In the beginning was the Word, and the Word was with God, and the Word was God.'[26] God is with Himself!"

With an even more extremely furrowed brow, Jesus asked, "How can God be separated from Himself?" Jesus paused for a moment. "While dying on the cross, the Son of God asked, 'My God, my God, why hast Thou forsaken me?'[27] God was separated from Himself."

"I think my brain has just disassembled," Cleopas jokingly complained.

---

17   2 Samuel 22:2-3
18   Luke 1:69
19   1 Corinthians 10:4
20   Psalm 132:11, 17
21   Psalm 18:2-3
22   Psalm 18:31
23   Psalm 18:35
24   Psalm 18:46
25   Psalm 19:14
26   John 1:1
27   Matthew 27:46

"Well, know this, my friend." Jesus put His hand on Cleopas' shoulder. "The psalmist saw this brain-disassembling conundrum many centuries before Jesus hung on that cross. He incredibly pictures the suffering Messiah when he declares 'My God, my God, why hast Thou forsaken me?'[28] Yes, with respect to the Trinity, the Son of God, became separated from Himself because of the sin that He bore.[29] The psalmist envisages the expression of this incredible, unfathomable cry one thousand years before its manifestation. The Son of God is seen in the Scriptures."

"Thinking of the cross again makes me realize how infuriated I was at the people who stood there mocking Jesus," Cleopas ruminated.

"Even this, my friend, is not something that the Scriptures did not see beforehand," Jesus explained. "The psalmist describes[30] how the people despise Jesus and sneer at Him on the cross in disgust as they 'wag the head' and as they mockingly scream out that He should deliver Himself or that God should deliver Him."[31]

"Yes!" Cleopas shouted. "This is exactly what infuriated me. What the psalmist wrote is exactly what those foolish people did. Jesus on the cross is seen in the Tanakh."

Jesus continued. "The Scriptures provide even a much more detailed picture of the crucifixion. Consider the psalm: 'My strength is dried up like a potsherd, and my tongue cleaves to my jaws; and You lay me in the dust of death. For dogs have surrounded me; a band of evildoers has encompassed me; they pierced my hands and my feet. I can count all my bones. They look, they stare at me; they divide my garments among them, and for my clothing they cast lots.'"[32]

Jonathan gasped. "This is exactly what happened three days ago. Yet, the psalmist envisages it one thousand years ago. He sees Christ's death on the

---

28   Psalm 22:1
29   2 Corinthians 5:21
30   Psalm 22:6-8
31   Matthew 27:39-43
32   Psalm 22:15-18

cross and describes how He was thirsty and how the soldiers cast lots for His clothing[33] after they had pierced His hands and feet[34] yet in such a way that none of His bones were broken;[35] thus, the soldiers did not need to break His bones to finish the deed. However, they did pierce His side.[36] He was crucified next to criminals.[37] His torturers gave Him gall and vinegar while He hung on the cross.[38] All of these things that were previously written about in the Scriptures came to pass.[39] Jesus is certainly seen in the Scriptures."

The bleating of sheep from down in the valley could be heard by those walking on the road. Pointing toward the sheep, Jesus asked Cleopas, "What is it that a shepherd actually does for his sheep?"

"The shepherd protects his sheep. He provides for them. He leads and guides them."

After a moment, to make sure he did not interrupt Cleopas, Jonathan added, "When necessary, the shepherd finds and restores the sheep."

"Yes," Jesus confirmed. "A shepherd does all of these things. The Good Shepherd also does all of these things for His sheep. The Messiah, Who is the Good Shepherd,[40] is referenced by the psalmist, who writes, 'The Lord is my shepherd, I shall not want. He makes me lie down in green pastures; He leads me beside quiet waters. He restores my soul; He guides me in the paths of righteousness for His name's sake.'[41] Jesus, the Good Shepherd, is seen in the Tanakh."

The sun was high in the sky. Its rays caused the damp tree branches to sparkle. A few wisps of clouds blended into the bright blue sky to display a sort of celestial soup. The majestic, rolling hills presented themselves as

---

33   Matthew 27:35
34   John 20:25-27
35   Psalm 34:20
36   Psalm 34:20; Zechariah 12:10
37   Psalm 22:16
38   Psalm 69:21
39   John 19:17-37
40   John 10:14; Hebrews 13:20
41   Psalm 23:1-3

if they were the focal point of a beautiful landscape painting. Jonathan stared out at the rolling hills. "The Creator is so creative. Surely, He made all things good."

"That Creator is the Word of God," Jesus inserted. "The psalmist writes, 'By the word of the Lord the heavens were made, and by the breath of His mouth all their host.'[42] The Son of God is seen in creation even as it was created through the Word of God. This Word of God is Jesus Himself.[43] Jesus is seen in the Psalms."

Jesus continued. "In fact, the psalmist references the pre-incarnate Christ, Who ultimately is the Person of the Trinity Who dwells with man and Who is often pictured in the Scriptures as 'the Angel of the Lord' Who, the psalmist says, 'encamps around those who fear Him, and rescues them.'[44] Christ's activities are described in the Scriptures."

"What was the worst day of your life?" Jonathan asked Cleopas.

"It was the same worst day of your life," Cleopas answered his friend.

"Yes . . . that very bad Friday just three days ago. They nailed His hands and His feet to that cross. In some ways, it seems as though it just happened an hour ago and in other ways, it seems like it happened ten years ago. In any case, unquestionably, that was the worst day of my life."

"It is a peculiar thing . . . crucifixion," Jesus concluded. "You have one man nailing another man's hands and feet into a piece of wood. Peculiar! Amazingly, as he refers to the way in which the Messiah dies on the cross, the psalmist writes about this peculiar thing: 'He keeps all his bones, not one of them is broken.'[45] They put the spikes just below His wrist bone so as to support the body's weight without ripping through the hand while He hung on the cross. No bones broken. Similarly, they nailed the spikes just above His heel bone.[46] No bones broken. They pierced Him in the side instead of

---

42   Psalm 33:6
43   John 1:1-3, 14
44   Psalm 34:7
45   Psalm 34:29
46   Genesis 3:15

breaking His legs.[47] No bones broken. And so, the psalmist points ahead to the crucified Messiah."[48]

"And those who condemned Him to death?" Cleopas rhetorically inquired.

"Yes. What about those who wrongfully accused Him and joined their hatred together to convict Him?" Jonathan looked at Jesus to see whether or not He would respond with anything from the Scriptures. "He was accused by false testimony,[49] and He was hated without a cause."[50]

Jesus responded. "The psalmist portrayed these people and their hateful actions toward the Messiah: 'Malicious witnesses rise up; they ask me of things that I do not know. They repay me evil for good, to the bereavement of my soul . . . But at my stumbling they rejoiced and gathered themselves together; the smiters whom I did not know gathered together against me, they slandered me without ceasing. Like godless jesters at a feast, they gnashed at me with their teeth . . . Do not let those who are wrongfully my enemies rejoice over me; nor let those who hate me without cause wink maliciously.'[51] Herein, Messiah is seen in the Scriptures.

"Jesus, the incarnate God, comes into the world to do God's will," the Teacher proclaimed with conviction. "As we are seeing, He is continuously seen in the Scriptures. The psalmist pictures the incarnation of the Son of God when he writes, 'Then I said, Behold, I come.'[52] This One Who comes then describes how He is seen in the Scriptures: 'In the scroll of the book it is written of me.' The Son of God comes to do God's will[53] and is seen in the Scriptures."

Cleopas was now thinking about something else. "Jonathan, what do you think about the whole Judas fiasco? How could he have betrayed the Master like that? Did you see that coming?"

---

47   John 19:31-34
48   Genesis 3:15
49   Mark 14:57
50   John 15:25
51   Psalm 35:11-12, 15-16, 19
52   Psalm 40:7
53   Psalm 40:8; Hebrews 10:7

"I don't think anyone saw that coming." Jonathan shook his head and clenched his teeth.

"Oh, but someone did see it coming," Jesus said knowingly.

"What do you mean, Teacher?" demanded Cleopas.

"The psalmist writes about Judas' betrayal of Christ, even after Judas sat around the table and ate with Him.[54] He says, 'Even my close friend in whom I trusted, who ate my bread, has lifted up his heel against me.'[55] Someone saw that coming. Christ is seen in the Scriptures even as the Scriptures see Christ. In fact," Jesus added, "The Scriptures see God the Father talking to God the Son."

"God is talking to God! This is another portrayal of the Trinity," Jonathan determined.

"The psalmist conveys such a scene: 'Your throne, O God, is forever and ever; a scepter of uprightness is the scepter of Your kingdom. You have loved righteousness and hated wickedness; therefore God, Your God, has anointed You.'[56] He then says, 'I will cause Thy name to be remembered in all generations; therefore, the peoples will give Thee thanks forever and ever.'[57] The Son of God is seen in the Scriptures."

"Teacher," Cleopas addressed Jesus, "please forgive me for such a question that I want to ask You now."

"You need no forgiveness for asking a question. Go ahead. What is your question?"

"Can a man save himself? I was once in Athens and I heard one of their philosophers say, 'There is no God who will save you. You must save yourself.' Is it true? Can a man save himself? Can a man be his own savior or redeemer?"

"Christ is the only Redeemer. His sacrifice is the only ransom.[58] No one can provide his own ransom.[59] Certainly, a man's works cannot save

---

54   Mark 14:18-20
55   Psalm 41:9
56   Psalm 45:6-7; Hebrews 1:8
57   Psalm 45:17
58   Mark 10:45
59   Ephesians 2:8

him,[60] for if they could then Christ died needlessly, and Christ did not die needlessly.[61] No! In fact, the salvation offered by Jesus comes with a very high price.[62] No man is able to pay that price, for it is a debt that can be satisfied only by God. God's payment does have an awesome result. Man can have eternal life."[63]

Jesus finished answering Cleopas' question. "The psalmist rejects your Athenian philosopher's assertion that 'you must save yourself.' The psalmist describes the nature of salvation when he writes, 'No man can by any means redeem his brother or give to God a ransom for him—for the redemption of his soul is costly, and he should cease trying forever—that he should live on eternally, that he should not undergo decay.'[64] Christ and His salvation are seen in the Tanakh."

Jesus looked up to the heavens. "Sometime soon, you will see the ascension of the Christ," promised Jesus. "The psalmist describes this ascension[65] when he writes, 'Why do you look with envy, O mountains with many peaks, at the mountain which God has desired for His abode? Surely the Lord will dwell there forever. The chariots of God are myriads, thousands upon thousands; the Lord is among them as at Sinai, in holiness. You have ascended on high, You have led captive Your captives; You have received gifts among men.'[66] Christ's ascension is seen in the Scriptures."

Jonathan was obviously in deep thought regarding something.

"What are you contemplating?" Jesus probed.

"I cannot stop thinking about Your statement: 'The salvation offered by Jesus comes with a very high price.' What is this price?"

Jesus responded with a question. "How much sin does an average person carry?"

---

60 Galatians 2:16
61 Galatians 2:20
62 1 Corinthians 6:20
63 John 3:16
64 Psalm 49:7-9
65 Mark 16:19; Acts 1:9-11
66 Psalm 68:16-18

"I know the wicked heart of man," offered Jonathan, "because I am one of those men, and I know my wicked heart. Even the average person carries an innumerable number of sins."

Jesus continued his line of questioning. "If you weighed all the sins of all the people on the earth that ever were or that ever will be, what would those sins weigh?"

"It would surely be immeasurable. Perhaps, it could only be said that it would be 'the weight of the world.'"

"Well said," Jesus congratulated Jonathan. "When Christ, Who knew no sin, became sin on behalf of others,[67] He certainly bore the weight of the world. He became a propitiation, a substitute; One Who paid the penalty yet did not commit the foul."

Jesus continued. "This picture of Christ and His salvation is painted by the psalmist, who writes, 'Those who hate me without a cause are more than the hairs of my head; those who would destroy me are powerful, being wrongfully my enemies; what I did not steal, I then have to restore.'[68] He continues his portrait when he points to the substitutionary death of the Messiah done as a propitiation for sin.[69] He writes, 'For zeal for Your house has consumed me, and the reproaches of those who reproach You have fallen on me.'[70] The Messiah's anger was exhibited in the temple because its rulers engaged in unjust, greedy practices within its courts.[71] The psalmist foresees the zeal that the Messiah has for His house and how it consumes Him. He also foresees the incredible price the Messiah pays for salvation. In so doing, the psalmist portrays the Messiah in the Scriptures."

"Now I have a question for you, Jonathan," Jesus announced. "We know that some people accepted Jesus, and some people rejected Him. What about His own brothers? How did Jesus' brothers respond to His ministry?"

---

67   2 Corinthians 5:21
68   Psalm 69:4
69   Romans 3:25
70   Psalm 69:9
71   John 2:13-17

For a few moments, Jonathan considered how to most diplomatically answer this question. "At least in the beginning, they did not believe in Him."[72]

"That is true. Nevertheless, the unexpected was actually expected. Long ago, the psalmist prophesied, 'I have become estranged from my brothers and an alien to my mother's sons.'[73] Even specific relationships that Jesus had are referenced in the Tanakh." Jesus added, "Details about the Messiah's relationships are seen in the Scriptures. So, too, are details about His crucifixion."

"I can give you details about His crucifixion," Jonathan offered somewhat reluctantly. "They gave Him wine mixed with gall to drink. After tasting it, He was unwilling to drink. When they had crucified Him, the scoundrels divided up His garments among themselves by casting lots."[74]

"Details," Jesus exclaimed. "The psalmists refer to these details in the same kind of detailed way. One psalmist writes, 'They also gave me gall for my food and for my thirst they gave me vinegar to drink.'[75] Another one writes, 'They divide my garments among them, and for my clothing they cast lots.'[76] Jesus and His crucifixion are clearly seen in the Tanakh."

Almost always being one step behind in the conversation, Cleopas revealed his pensive wanderings when he asked, "The Scriptures reference those who would reject Christ, but do they not also reference those who would accept Him?"

"Yes, people like us." Jonathan put his arm around Cleopas, smiling at him almost as if he knew he needed some encouragement at that moment.

"The Scriptures say quite a bit, in fact, about the followers of Christ," Jesus confirmed. "While referencing those who worship the Savior, the psalmist writes, 'Let them fear You while the sun endures, and as long as the moon, throughout all generations. May he come down like rain upon the mown grass, like showers that water the earth. In his days may the righteous flourish, and

---

72 John 7:5
73 Psalm 69:8
74 Matthew 27:34-35
75 Psalm 69:21
76 Psalm 22:18

abundance of peace till the moon is no more.'[77] This is the One, the psalmist says, who will 'rule from sea to sea . . . to the ends of the earth.'[78] All kings will bow down before Him and all nations will serve Him.[79] His name will endure forever[80] for 'the lives of the needy he will save.'[81] The Messiah and His followers are seen in the Scriptures.

"Follow me," Jesus instructed the two men as He walked off the road and toward the brow of the hill. Cleopas and Jonathan followed Him. Pointing down the hill, Jesus inquired, "Do you see the small fire that is made for burning the rubbish and the small pool of water that sits just beyond it?"

"Yes, Teacher," responded Jonathan. "It is right there."

"Which is more powerful, the fire or the water?"

"The fire," Cleopas answered definitively.

"No," Jonathan disagreed. "I would say the water is more powerful."

"One day, the fire and the water began to rage; the fire spreading and the water flowing. Suddenly, the fire ran into the water and the water ran into the fire. Up rose an enormous plume of holy mist that made its way toward the heavens. Meanwhile, the power of both the fire and the water were diminished significantly."

"The follower of Christ must be able to say, 'He must increase, but I must decrease.'"[82]

"You are now speaking in parables," Cleopas announced.

"Yes, even as Jesus did when He was with us," Jonathan reminisced.

"And even as the psalmist pictured Him doing," Jesus inserted as He established the point being made.

"Details," Jesus said firmly, yet in such a way as to promote reflection. "Even the teaching style of the Messiah is mentioned in the Tanakh. Jesus

---

77 Psalm 72:5-7; Isaiah 24:23; Revelation 21:23
78 Psalm 72:8; Luke 1:32-33
79 Psalm 72:11; Revelation 12:10
80 Psalm 72:17; Hebrews 13:21
81 Psalm 72:13; Mark 2:17; Matthew 5:3
82 John 3:30

often spoke in parables,[83] and the psalmist points to that fact as he writes down God's declaration, 'Listen, O my people, to my instruction; incline your ears to the words of my mouth. I will open my mouth in a parable.'[84] Jesus. Parables. Details."

A few drops of rain fell on the travelers who were walking on the road. "Like this rain, the manna given in the wilderness came raining down from the heavens," Jesus asserted. "The psalmist mentions this manna as it serves as a type of Christ. 'He commanded the clouds above and opened the doors of heaven; He rained down manna upon them to eat and gave them food from heaven.'[85] Even as God fed the people in the wilderness His manna from Heaven—having opened the doors of Heaven—so, too, did Christ come out of heaven[86] to the people in the wilderness.[87] The manna is a type of Christ seen in the Scriptures. He is the Bread of Life."[88]

Jesus continued. "He is the Bread of Life and He is the Vine. God the Son is the Vine, and God the Father is the Vinedresser.[89] The Son of God sits at the right hand of the Father.[90] The Son of Man shines His face upon His people and brings His salvation to them.[91] The psalmist paints all these same pictures. The Son of Man is pictured, by the psalmist, as the Vine Who is cared for by God the Father, the Vinedresser.[92] He is the Son Who is at the right hand of God.[93] It is this Son of Man Who will bring salvation as His face shines upon His people.[94] The Son of Man is seen in the Tanakh.

"Let us ponder." Jesus stopped in the road, just standing there gently nodding His head. "What is the single most miraculous event in all of history?"

---

83   Matthew 13:3
84   Psalm 78:1-2
85   Psalm 78:23-24
86   John 3:13
87   Matthew 3:1
88   John 6:35
89   John 15:1
90   Mark 16:19
91   2 Corinthians 4:6
92   Psalm 80:14
93   Psalm 80:15, 17
94   Psalm 80:19

Cleopas jumped in immediately. "It must be when Jesus calmed the storm."[95]

Jonathan took his turn. "The feeding of the five thousand.[96] Think about it, Cleopas—five thousand people, and that's not even counting the women and the children. I mean, come on! There were only five loaves and two fish. And then there were twelve baskets of pieces leftover. Come on! Who feeds five thousand with a few loaves and a few fish and has leftovers?"

Jesus gently redirected the conversation. "Of course, both of your answers are reasonable. Nevertheless, neither one is the single most miraculous event in history. That honor is reserved for, perhaps, the most unpredictable of answers—that is, the birth of a baby. The most miraculous event is that God Himself came to man. God became a Man. The most miraculous event is His coming, His incarnation."

"This great miracle of the incarnation of the Son of God is seen throughout the Scriptures. One such reference is supplied by the psalmist when he writes, 'Before the Lord, for He is coming, for He is coming to judge the earth. He will judge the world in righteousness and the peoples in His faithfulness.'[97] Again, the psalmist writes, 'for He is coming to judge the earth'[98] and 'the Lord has made known His salvation; He has revealed His righteousness in the sight of the nations . . . all the ends of the earth have seen the salvation of our God.'[99] Truly, His miraculous coming is seen in the Tanakh."

Jonathan asked his own question now. "Is there anything more fundamental regarding the description of Christ in the Scriptures than Him being seen as the Savior?"

"You are right Jonathan," affirmed Jesus. "Christ is most definitively associated with salvation. When you see salvation in the Scriptures, you see Christ, for He is the Savior."

---

95   Matthew 8:23-27
96   Matthew 14:18-21
97   Psalm 96:13
98   Psalm 98:9
99   Psalm 98:2-3

"And so, the psalmist references 'God their Savior.'[100] Throughout the Scriptures, God is the Savior. The prophet writes, 'My God, my rock, in whom I take refuge, my shield and the horn of my salvation, my stronghold and my refuge; my savior.'[101] These references point to Jesus Christ 'for today in the city of David there has been born for you a Savior, who is Christ the Lord.'[102] 'So when the Samaritans came to Jesus . . . they were saying . . . we have heard for ourselves and know that this One is indeed the Savior of the world.'[103] Salvation is 'according to His own purpose and grace which was granted us in Christ Jesus from all eternity, but now has been revealed by the appearing of our Savior Christ Jesus.'[104]

"God the Savior referenced by the psalmist and the prophet has now become visible 'for the grace of God has appeared, bringing salvation to all men . . . looking for the blessed hope and the appearing of the glory of our great God and Savior, Christ Jesus.'[105] This Savior is God: 'But when the kindness of God our Savior and His love for mankind appeared, He saved us, not on the basis of deeds which we have done in righteousness, but according to His mercy, by the washing of regeneration and renewing by the Holy Spirit, whom He poured out upon us richly through Jesus Christ our Savior.'[106] He is 'our God and Savior, Jesus Christ.'[107] And so, we see Jesus Christ our Savior in the Scriptures."

Jonathan stopped on the road. In a moment of spontaneous worship, he lifted his arms and proclaimed, "Our God and Savior is full of mercy. His lovingkindness endures forever. He intercedes even for His enemies."

"It is true!" Cleopas contributed with a measure of amazement in his voice. "Jesus prayed even for those who acted as His torturers. The Messiah, while being tortured, asked the Father to forgive His torturers."[108]

---

100 Psalm 106:21
101 2 Samuel 22:3
102 Luke 2:11
103 John 4:40-42
104 2 Timothy 1:9-10
105 Titus 2:11, 13
106 Titus 3:4-6
107 2 Peter 1:1
108 Luke 23:34

Jesus further explained. "The psalmist anticipates the mercy of the Son of God who prays for His enemies: 'They have also surrounded me with words of hatred, and fought against me without cause. In return for my love they act as my accusers; but I am in prayer.'[109] The merciful Son of God is seen in the Tanakh."

"Not everyone and not every action is shown mercy," Cleopas half-asserted and half-inquired.

"Definitely," agreed Jonathan. "I am thinking of Judas and his betrayal of the Lord."

Jesus, with anything but exuberance, concurred. "Judas did not receive mercy,[110] and his office was taken from him and given to another.[111] The psalmist foresees this and writes, 'Appoint a wicked man over him, and let an accuser stand at his right hand. When he is judged, let him come forth guilty, and let his prayer become sin. Let his days be few; let another take his office.'[112] Christ is seen in the Scriptures."

"So many questions," pondered Cleopas.

"Questions can be good," countered Jesus.

Jonathan remembered, "Yes, but it came to a point with Jesus that 'no one was able to answer Him a word, nor did anyone dare from that day on to ask Him another question.'[113] This was after He challenged the Pharisees with respect to His identity as He quoted from the psalm that says that the Lord says to my Lord, 'Sit at My right hand until I make Your enemies a footstool for Your feet.'"[114]

Jesus added, "Of course, the psalmist, here, paints a picture of the Trinity and, in so doing, declares Jesus' divinity and authority.[115] At the same time, the psalmist points to the ascension of Christ that is still to come."[116]

---

109 Psalm 109:3-4
110 Matthew 27:3-5
111 Acts 1:20
112 Psalm 109:6-8
113 Matthew 22:46
114 Psalm 110:1
115 Acts 2:34-36; Hebrews 1:1-4, 13
116 Mark 16:19

Just then, a priest passed them by on the other side of the road. Jonathan stared at him for a few moments until he was out of sight. "Is not the Christ also a Priest?" inquired Jonathan.

"Yes, He is, Jonathan," answered Jesus. "In fact, the psalmist writes of a situation in which God is speaking to God, and God the Father says to God the Son, 'You are a priest forever according to the order of Melchizedek.'[117] Indeed, Christ is the High Priest,[118] and Melchizedek is a type of the Son of God as He is 'without father, without mother, without genealogy, having neither beginning of days nor end of life, but made like the Son of God, he remains a priest perpetually.'[119] In this enigmatic way, the Son of God is seen in the Tanakh."

Still looking back in the other direction, Jonathan muttered, "Where is that priest going?"

"To Jerusalem," Cleopas stated matter-of-factly.

"Are not the priests our leaders? Are not the Pharisees our builders?" Jonathan scoffed.

Cleopas let out a growl. "What irony! It is the Pharisee who condemned Jesus. It is the builder who tore Him down."

Jesus took Jonathan's shoulder and turned him around as He motioned him to walk facing forward again. "The psalmist prophesies of these builders, 'The stone which the builders rejected has become the chief corner stone. This is the Lord's doing; it is marvelous in our eyes.'[120] The Pharisees rejected Christ. They were trying to build a house of faith, but they discarded the very cornerstone that is used to build that house. Jesus references that psalm as He tells a parable to the Pharisees about their rejection of Him and then identifies Himself as the Cornerstone over Who they stumble.'[121] Jesus is seen in the Scriptures."

---

117   Psalm 110:1, 4; Hebrews 5:5-6
118   Hebrews 3:1
119   Hebrews 7:3
120   Psalm 118:22-23
121   Isaiah 8:15; Matthew 21:42

CHAPTER 13

CONVERSING IN PROVERBS, JOB, SONG OF SONGS

Up ahead on the other side of the road and just down the hill was a stream. "I am thirsty. How about you two?" Cleopas asked his friends.

Jonathan cleared his throat. "I think it is time for some water. Let's go down there and join the other travelers who are refreshing themselves."

The three men made their way down to the stream. They knelt down and began to drink.

Jesus playfully splashed some water on Jonathan and then on Cleopas. "Do you remember what Jesus said He would do with the Spirit?"

Jonathan responded immediately, almost as though he anticipated the question. "He said He would send the Spirit to us."[1]

"Exactly!" Jesus took another drink of water. "The writer of Proverbs anticipated this blessed event when he wrote, 'Turn to my reproof, behold, I will pour out my spirit on you; I will make my words known to you.'[2] Even Jesus' pouring out of the Spirit is seen in the Tanakh."

Obviously excited over the thought of having the Spirit poured out upon him, Jonathan exclaimed, "I long for the Spirit to be poured out. Oh, might the wisdom of God be my portion."

---

1   John 16:7
2   Proverbs 1:23

"Know this. When wisdom falls upon you, it is nothing less than God Himself falling upon you," Jesus instructed.

"The writer of Proverbs refers to the incarnate Christ—Who is Wisdom—as He personifies wisdom and pictures it in its perfection. Wisdom is clearly seen as a foundational aspect of the character of God.[3] It is to be obeyed, and through it, life can be found: 'Blessed is the man who listens to me, watching daily at my gates, waiting at my doorposts. For he who finds me finds life.'[4] Wisdom becomes incarnate in Christ 'in whom are hidden all the treasures of wisdom and knowledge.'[5] Christ Jesus became 'wisdom from God' to those who believe.[6] The 'wisdom picture' painted in Proverbs points to Jesus." Jesus looked up. "What a picture!"

"What are you seeing, Teacher," asked Jonathan.

"Look at those boys playing over there by the hill. They are running down the hill and then turning right around and running up the hill. The Son of God ran down the hill. He descended to become a Man. Then He ran back up the hill. He ascended to be seated at the right hand of God the Father."

"And as you have shown us," agreed Jonathan, "Christ's incarnation and ascension are seen in the Law and the Prophets."

"Yes," added Jesus, "and they are also seen in the Writings."

"The writer of Proverbs, for example, depicts the incarnation and ascension of the Son of God. 'Neither have I learned wisdom, nor do I have the knowledge of the Holy One. Who has ascended into heaven and descended? Who has gathered the wind in His fists? Who has wrapped the waters in His garment? Who has established all the ends of the earth? What is His name or His son's name? Surely you know!'[7] It is the Holy One, the One Who established all the ends of the earth, Who has ascended and descended for 'no one has ascended into heaven, but He who descended from heaven:

---

3   Proverbs 8:22-31
4   Proverbs 8:34-35
5   Colossians 2:3
6   1 Corinthians 1:30
7   Proverbs 30:3-4

the Son of Man.'[8] And so Jesus—the Son of God and the Son of Man—is seen in the Scriptures."

Jesus continued. "Job sees a glorious picture of the coming Messiah. He proclaims that his Divine Redeemer is yet to come: 'As for me, I know that my Redeemer lives, and at the last He will take His stand on the earth. Even after my skin is destroyed, yet from my flesh I shall see God; whom I myself shall behold, and whom my eyes will see and not another.'[9] Job declares that he will see the Son of Man, Who will be his ransom.[10] He speaks of a Mediator Who says, 'Deliver him from going down to the pit, I have found a ransom.'[11] Job then says of man, 'He will pray to God, and He will accept him, that he may see His face with joy, and He may restore His righteousness to man.'[12] The Son of Man is seen in the Tanakh."

"Tell me more about yourself, Cleopas," Jesus insisted. "Where were you born? How old are you?"

"I was born in Emmaus twenty-nine years ago."

"And you, Jonathan."

"I was born in Emmaus almost thirty-five years ago."

"Oh, what a glorious day when Christ was born in Bethlehem thirty-three years ago," Jesus exclaimed.

"The Christ-child is seen in God's rebuke of Job. God lists off the things that Job cannot do en route to challenging and correcting Job's presumptuous and misguided conclusions about God's error in matters pertaining to Job's suffering. One of the things that Job cannot do is make 'the wild ox consent to serve you' or make it 'spend the night at your manger.'[13] Of course, Job, who is but a man, cannot do this. But God, Who is the Almighty, can cause His creations, the animals, to worship Him even at His manger, along with

---

8   John 3:13
9   Job 19:25-27
10   Mark 10:45
11   Job 33:24
12   Job 33:26
13   Job 39:9

the shepherds and their flocks at His birth in Bethlehem.[14] And so, the Christ is seen in the Scriptures in this very specific way."

Far ahead, on the other side of the road, a loud commotion was brewing. "What is going on up there?" Cleopas inquired.

"I can't tell," admitted Jonathan. "It's too far away. But it does look like there are people who are coming toward us. There seems to be quite a crowd."

As he squinted until his eyes were almost fully shut, Cleopas was able to identify something. "It must be a marriage procession. I see the bride being carried on a small bed. She has a crown on her head."

Finally, the procession reached the place in the road where Jesus, Cleopas, and Jonathan were walking. They, like everyone else, moved off to the side to make way for this very celebratory marriage procession. There were musicians and many friends and relatives who were walking and dancing and throwing flowers on the ground. It was quite a party.

"I think they're happy," Cleopas muttered in his best deadpan manner of understatement.

"I think they're more than happy," Jonathan modified Cleopas' understated statement. "There is a bride, and there is a groom; there is love!"

Jesus entered the conversation. "There is no greater picture of this than what is painted in the Song of Songs. There, Solomon anticipates the coming Christ as he portrays Israel as the bride[15] that precedes the Church as the Bride.[16] The Bride of Christ, then, is seen in the Song of Songs as being enamored with Christ.[17] Christ is seen throughout the Scriptures, including in the Song of Songs, as the Lover of His people.[18] Christ is even seen in the Song of Songs as the Husband Who says, 'You have made my heart beat faster, my sister, my bride.'[19] And so, the beating heart of Jesus for His people[20] is seen in the Scriptures."

---

14   Luke 2:15-20
15   Isaiah 54:5-6
16   2 Corinthians 11:2
17   Song of Songs 1:2-4
18   Song of Songs 4:1-16
19   Song of Songs 4:9
20   Philippians 1:8; Matthew 23:37

Jesus continued. "The bride and the husband are seen in the Song of Songs as being 'one.' The bride proclaims, 'I am my beloved's and my beloved is mine.'[21] Of course, Christ and His Church—His bride—are 'one.'[22] Moreover, Christ, the Divine Bridegroom[23] is the bride's Maker.[24] Here, then, we see Christ and His Church in the Tanakh."

---

21   Song of Solomon 6:3
22   Romans 12:5; 2 Corinthians 5:17; Ephesians 5:32
23   Matthew 9:14-15
24   Isaiah 54:5

CHAPTER 14

CONVERSING IN RUTH, LAMENTATIONS, ECCLESIASTES

"Tell me more about yourself, Jonathan," suggested Jesus. "Who are your relatives?"

"My father and mother are Simeon and Martha. My wife is Sarah. We have five children—Samuel, Nathan, John, Sapphira, and Salome. I have two brothers, Ananias and Lazarus. My uncle is Joseph."

Jesus nodded His head. "What about you, Cleopas? Who are your closest kin?"

"My father and mother are Judas and Imma. My wife is Joanna. We have two children—Mary and Berenice. My brothers are Matthew, Simon, and Joses. My uncles are James, Levi, Bartimaeus, Simeon, and John."

"So those are your kin," Jesus acknowledged. "What is a kinsman redeemer?"

Cleopas offered an answer. "A kinsman redeemer is one who acts on behalf of a relative who is in trouble, or in danger, or in need. That redeemer, then, is to redeem the situation."

Jesus nodded in agreement. "Christ is the Son of God, Who redeems man.[1] He is the ultimate Kinsman Redeemer, Who redeems the whole world.[2] He is foreshadowed in the scroll of Ruth as is consistent with the work of the

---

1   Galatians 4:5
2   John 3:16

kinsman redeemer. Boaz, a type of Christ, redeems Naomi as he is her blood relative who is able[3] and willing[4] to pay the price of redemption. He becomes her kinsman redeemer. Similarly, Jesus Christ is connected by blood to those whom He redeems.[5] He is both able[6] and willing[7] to redeem. And so, one thousand years before Jesus died on the cross, He and His redemptive work are seen via the kinsman redeemer in the Scriptures. In addition, the child born to the redeemed one via the redeemer, Boaz, was named Obed. Obed became the grandfather of David through whose line came the Redeemer, the Christ."[8]

Surprisingly, just as there had been a marriage procession just a short time ago, now there was a funeral procession making its way down the road. This time, of course, there was no celebration. There was no dancing. There was only weeping and wailing.

Jonathan looked away. "I cannot bear to look at those who are mourning and weeping."

Jesus approached Jonathan on the side of the road. He placed His hands on both shoulders. "I understand, Jonathan. No one likes to see the expression of the fallen world. Nevertheless, it is sometimes necessary to stare in the face of lament. It is important to look at the prophet Jeremiah."

"Jeremiah is not weeping," Jonathan challenged Jesus.

Jesus stared into Jonathan's eyes. "Actually, Jeremiah is the weeper, as is Christ. In the scroll of Lamentations, Jeremiah serves as a type of Christ. He weeps over Jerusalem as he identifies with human suffering caused by sin.[9] Six hundred years later, God, in the Person of Christ, would weep over the same city in the same way.[10] Jeremiah's ministry points to Christ's ministry

---

3   Ruth 2:1
4   Ruth 3:11
5   Hebrews 2:14-15; Matthew 26:28
6   1 Peter 1:18-19
7   Matthew 20:28
8   Ruth 4:17
9   Lamentations 1:16-18
10   Matthew 23:37-38

as they both are men of sorrows who are acquainted with grief.[11] Jeremiah, like Christ, is severely afflicted:[12] 'Is it nothing to all you who pass this way? Look and see if there is any pain like my pain which was severely dealt out to me, which the Lord inflicted on the day of His fierce anger.'[13]

"Jeremiah, like Christ, is despised, scorned, mocked, and tormented by his enemies.[14] 'All who pass along the way clap their hands in derision at you; they hiss and shake their heads . . . all your enemies have opened their mouths wide against you; they hiss and gnash their teeth.'[15] And so, Christ is seen in Lamentations in the person of Jeremiah. He was mocked, spit on, scourged, and tortured.[16] Jesus bore the sin of men in His body on the cross so that by His affliction and pain they might be healed.[17] Jesus is seen in the Scriptures."

"Tell me, Cleopas," requested Jesus, "Why do the Scriptures say that it is a fool who says, 'There is no God'?"[18]

"They are fools because in saying 'there is no God,' they actually negate themselves."

"That is quite true," agreed Jonathan. "The proof of God's existence is built right into the very nature of man."

Cleopas repeated, "When a man negates the existence of God, he negates himself."

Cleopas continued. "Man is aware of the eternal. He cannot fully comprehend or explain it, but he is aware of it. There is something about the way God made man—with eternity in his heart—that prompts him to want to know the eternal One,[19] not to negate Him."

---

11   Isaiah 53:3
12   Lamentations 3:19
13   Lamentations 1:12
14   Lamentations 3:14, 30
15   Lamentations 2:15-16
16   Mark 10:34
17   1 Peter 2:23-24
18   Psalm 14:1
19   Hosea 6:3

Jesus smiled. "This is where Christ comes into the equation. He is pointed to in the scroll of Ecclesiastes when the Preacher asserts, 'He has also set eternity in their heart, yet so that man will not find out the work which God has done from the beginning even to the end.'[20] Man is made with the awareness of eternity inside of him. Eternal life is to know Jesus Christ.[21] God has set eternity in man's heart; thus, He has set a hunger to know Christ in man's heart. In this way, the Preacher points to Jesus.

"The Preacher points to Christ again," Jesus continued. "Jesus, the Good Shepherd, is referenced by the Preacher when he declares, 'The words of wise men are like goads, and masters of these collections are like well-driven nails; they are given by one Shepherd.'[22] The wise and caring One is the Good Shepherd, Who knows His sheep and lays down His life for them.[23] This is none other than the Messiah, the Son of God, to Whom the Preacher refers in the Scriptures."

---

20 Ecclesiastes 3:11
21 John 17:3
22 Ecclesiastes 12:11
23 John 10:14-15

CHAPTER 15

CONVERSING IN ESTHER, DANIEL

"What do you think? Who is the opposite of the Good Shepherd?" Jesus threw out a seemingly random question.

"Is this a loaded question?" Jonathan snickered.

"Or perhaps, it's a riddle or the beginning of a bad joke?" Cleopas chuckled.

Jesus smiled. "It is not a joke, nor a riddle, nor a loaded question. It is a history question."

"Well, who is the opposite of the Good Shepherd?" Cleopas returned the question to the Teacher.

"The opposite of the Good Shepherd is the evil thief. This, of course, is the devil. He is the one who steals, kills, and destroys.[1] He deceives, oppresses, devours and, ultimately, tries to destroy the Christ-child.[2] In fact, throughout the Scriptures, the evil thief is seen as trying to destroy the Jewish people, and thus, eradicate the Messianic line. The Good Shepherd, however, stands in the way. The scroll of Esther depicts one of the times in which God thwarts an attempt at disrupting His ultimate plan.[3] Haman, full of the wickedness of the evil thief, births a plan to bring about the genocide of the Jewish people.[4] Esther points to the Messiah in that she is used to spoil Haman's plan and,

---

1   John 10:10
2   Revelation 12:9; Acts 10:38; 1 Peter 5:8; Matthew 2:13
3   Esther 8:4-17
4   Esther 3:6

thus, preserve the Messianic line. Beyond this, she portrays the Messiah's willingness to offer His life on behalf of the people[5] and, in so doing, portrays Christ's work as Advocate for deliverance from sin and evil.[6] Herein, Christ is seen in the Writings."

Staring off to the side of the road, Jonathan remarked, "Look at the children playing. They are so innocent and carefree. If I could only be like a child . . . "

"You must be like a child," Cleopas emphasized. "Remember Jesus' words when He was with us: 'Truly I say to you, whoever does not receive the kingdom of God like a child will not enter it at all.'"[7]

"Teacher, when will the Kingdom of God come?" Jonathan asked sincerely.

"The Kingdom is come, and the Kingdom is yet to come. The Kingdom is already, and the Kingdom is not yet. The Kingdom is seen long ago. When Daniel interprets Nebuchadnezzar's dream, he describes the Kingdom of God that will be ushered in by the coming Messiah, the 'Stone.'[8] 'In the days of those kings, the God of Heaven will set up a kingdom which will never be destroyed, and that kingdom will not be left for another people; it will crush and put an end to all these kingdoms, but it will itself endure forever. Inasmuch as you saw that a stone was cut out of the mountain without hands and that it crushed the iron, the bronze, the clay, the silver and the gold, the great God has made known to the king what will take place in the future.'[9] The future Messiah is seen in the Scriptures.

"Let's have another history lesson," Jesus suggested. "What people and ruler took Judah into captivity?"

Cleopas jumped in quickly, so as to be the first to answer. "That would be the Babylonians and King Nebuchadnezzar."

Jesus nodded. "And who were put into the fiery furnace because they refused to worship the golden image?"

---

5   Esther 4:15-17; Mark 9:31
6   Esther 7:1-4; 1 John 2:1
7   Mark 10:15-16
8   Matthew 21:42-44
9   Daniel 2:44-45

Again, Cleopas answered quickly, "Shadrach, Meshach, and Abednego."

Clapping His hands to applaud him, Jesus declared, "You are a very good history student, Cleopas."

"He is a very fast-talking history student," Jonathan complained somewhat bitterly.

Jesus waited for a few moments as if to give Jonathan a little bit of time to think about what he had just said. "Just as God delivered Daniel from the mouths of the lions, so, too, He delivered Shadrach, Meshach, and Abednego from the flames of the fire. It was the Son of God Who walked about in the blazing fire and delivered them. Nebuchadnezzar was amazed when he saw that the three men were not incinerated and that there was a fourth Man walking around in the furnace with them. He said, 'Look! I see four men loosed and walking about in the midst of the fire without harm, and the appearance of the fourth is like a son of the gods!'[10] The Son of God is seen in the Scriptures, even if it is in the most unorthodox of places."

Jonathan's bitter heart caught up with him, and he was truly repentant. "Teacher, forgive me for my selfish outburst. Cleopas, forgive me for my jealous heart toward you."

Both Jesus and Cleopas immediately reassured Jonathan of their forgiveness.

At once, Jonathan fell onto his knees and prayed, "Our Father who is in heaven, hallowed be Your name. Your kingdom come. Your will be done, on earth as it is in heaven. Give us this day our daily bread. And forgive us our debts."[11]

"Jonathan," Jesus proclaimed, "you are not far from the Kingdom of God."[12]

Jonathan rose up, and the three men began to walk down the road again.

Jesus affirmed, "That is a valuable prayer . . . 'Your Kingdom come.' In a vision, Daniel sees Christ as the Son of Man in all His glory. He is presented

---

10 Daniel 3:25
11 Matthew 6:9-12
12 Mark 12:34

as the One Who has an eternal kingdom and Who stands as the authority over all power and dominion.[13] Daniel writes, 'I kept looking in the night visions, and behold, with the clouds of heaven One like a Son of Man was coming, and He came up to the Ancient of Days and was presented before Him. And to Him was given dominion, glory and a kingdom, that all the peoples, nations and men of every language might serve Him. His dominion is an everlasting dominion which will not pass away; and His kingdom is one which will not be destroyed.'[14] The Son of Man and His kingdom are seen in the Tanakh."

"Daniel certainly saw incredible visions of Christ," Cleopas said.

Jesus agreed. "Daniel sees a vision of the coming Savior, the Prince.[15] This 'Messiah the Prince' and 'Prince of princes' will be opposed by an evil ruler.[16] In this vision, even the crucifixion of the Christ—He is 'opposed' and 'cut off'—is seen in the Scriptures.[17] In addition, there is a prophecy about the destruction of Jerusalem and its temple: 'Then after the sixty-two weeks the Messiah will be cut off and have nothing, and the people of the prince who is to come will destroy the city and the sanctuary.'[18] Again, the Messiah is seen in the Tanakh."

Jesus stopped in the middle of the road and crouched down to be able to write.

Cleopas hit Jonathan on the arm as if to say, "Here He goes again."

Jesus drew in the dirt.

Jonathan bent down to get a closer look.

"What does it say?" Cleopas asked.

Jonathan looked up at him. "He has written the number '70' in the dirt."

"Yes, I have." Jesus broke up the awkwardness.

"Tell us what '70' signifies," pleaded Jonathan.

---

13 Ephesians 1:20-22
14 Daniel 7:13-14
15 Acts 5:31
16 Daniel 8:25; Acts 3:14-15
17 Daniel 9:26
18 Daniel 9:25-26

Jesus stood up. "In Daniel's prophecy concerning when the Messiah would come, he describes the atoning ministry of Christ through the work of the cross that would bring an end to the power of sin and result in everlasting righteousness. This is why the Son of God came into the world, to offer atonement for iniquity,[19] to gain victory over sin,[20] and to offer eternal life.[21] And so, Daniel prophesies, 'Seventy weeks have been decreed for your people and your holy city, to finish the transgression, to make an end of sin, to make atonement for iniquity, to bring in everlasting righteousness.'"[22]

Jesus again stooped down and drew in the dirt. He wrote the number '70' again, but this time, He also drew a cross next to it. He stood up and turned to the two men. "Seventy weeks and then . . . atonement for iniquity that will be finalized at the second coming of Christ when all will be completed and perfected; thus, the perfect number, '70.' The Messiah, His salvation, and His second coming are seen in the Tanakh."

"Yes, I see Him now, Teacher," Jonathan cried.

"I believe you do," Jesus said matter-of-factly.

"Do you remember, Jonathan," probed Cleopas, "how Jesus so clearly claimed to be the Messiah when he conversed with the Samaritan woman at Jacob's well?"

"Yes, I remember. She said to Him, 'I know that Messiah is coming, He who is called Christ; when that One comes, He will declare all things to us.'[23] Then Jesus said to her, 'I who speak to you am He.'"[24]

Jesus spoke up. "Jesus is the Messiah. Daniel prophesies of His coming as he establishes a 483-year time period that would extend from the decree to rebuild Jerusalem and end with the coming of 'Messiah the Prince.'[25] From

---

19   Romans 3:25
20   1 Corinthians 15:56-57
21   John 3:16
22   Daniel 9:24
23   John 4:25
24   John 4:26
25   Daniel 9:25

the time that King Artaxerxes issued that decree to Ezra the priest[26] to the time that the Messiah began His ministry,[27] it was 483 years. This prophecy was made over four hundred years before Christ, yet it is accurate down to the exact year. The Messiah is seen in the Tanakh."

Jesus continued. "Daniel had a vision of the pre-incarnate Christ.[28] This was One who, although having human appearance,[29] 'His body also was like beryl, his face had the appearance of lightning, his eyes were like flaming torches, his arms and feet like the gleam of polished bronze, and the sound of his words like the sound of a tumult.'[30] Who is this splendid, majestic 'Man' Whom Daniel sees. This is the Christ, the God-Man; He is the 'God who can be seen.'[31] Daniel's vision is a vision of Christ in the Scriptures."

---

26   Ezra 7:11-26; 457 B.C.
27   Matthew 3:16; 4:17
28   Daniel 10:4-21
29   Daniel 10:5, 16, 18; Philippians 2:7
30   Daniel 10:6
31   Revelation 1:12-16

CHAPTER 16

CONVERSING IN EZRA, NEHEMIAH, CHRONICLES

They walked downhill for most of their journey. The fog that covered the horizon started to lift. There it was.

"Emmaus!" shouted Jonathan. "We are certainly no further than one thousand cubits away."

"The seven mile journey went by especially fast this time. It must have been because of our conversations with the Teacher," concluded Cleopas.

Jonathan shook his head in agreement. "In any case, it's only a small journey. On the other hand," Jonathan paused, "I can't even imagine how long the journey was that the Israelites took when they returned to Jerusalem after the decree given by Artaxerxes on behalf of Ezra."

"That journey," asserted Cleopas knowingly, "would be about nine hundred miles."

Acting like he was weighing two different things in his hands, Jonathan chuckled. "Babylon to Jerusalem or Jerusalem to Emmaus."

Cleopas put his arm around his friend and pointed joyfully toward their village. "We'll take Jerusalem to Emmaus every time."

Jesus walked a few paces in front of them. "Speaking of Ezra, the exile in Babylon, and the return to Jerusalem, the sovereignty of God can be seen in the Scriptures. Ezra reports that 'the Lord stirred up the spirit of Cyrus king of Persia[1] to release the Israelites from bondage in Babylon and allow them to return to Jerusalem to reestablish Israel.[2] This is very important with respect to the plan of salvation. The Messiah would be born in Bethlehem,[3] not in Babylon! Thus, the particular history of the Christ is seen in the events of Scripture."

Jesus continued. "The particular history of the Christ is represented by His genealogy. Thus, as in many places in the Scriptures, the Christ is seen in the continued fulfillment of the promise to carry on the line of David from which would come the Son of God.[4] Zerubbabel, the son of Shealtiel,[5] the son of Jeconiah[6] was in the Messianic line.[7] Zerubbabel lived five hundred years before Christ, and thus, he portrays Christ's lineage up until the very end of the events in the Tanakh. And so, Christ's genealogy is prophesied and preserved throughout the Scriptures."

Jonathan excitedly pointed ahead. "Look, Cleopas, it's your brother, Joses, running toward us."

"How can you tell it is Joses?" Cleopas probed while he squinted his eyes and tried to get a clearer look.

Jonathan let out a hearty laugh. "Even from this distance, I can tell it is Joses just by the way he runs."

Cleopas laughed along with Jonathan. "You know, I tried to help him since he was just a boy. He has run like that since I can remember. He's just not very coordinated."

"His legs are considerably spread apart from each other, and his arms are lifted up and out to his side; yet he is actually able to run like that," Jonathan exclaimed in amazement. "Who runs like that?"

"My brother Joses does," Cleopas countered. "That's why we call him 'the Spider.'"

---

1   Ezra 1:1
2   Ezra 1:2-3
3   Micah 5:2
4   Isaiah 9:7
5   Ezra 3:2
6   1 Chronicles 3:17
7   Matthew 1:12-17

Just then, Joses caught up to them. The laughter stopped as Cleopas, and then Jonathan hugged him, and the men exchanged joyous greetings.

"Oh, forgive me, Teacher," Cleopas apologized looking over at Jesus. "This is my youngest brother, Joses."

"Greetings, Joses." Jesus smiled. "Your big brother, Cleopas, speaks very highly of you."

Hearing the playfulness in Jesus' voice, Joses looked at Cleopas with a partial smirk on his face. "So, what have you been saying about me now?"

"Nothing you don't say about yourself. I commented on your special running style and how we call you the Spider."

"Of course!" Joses chuckled. "You're just jealous that you can't run like a spider. Have you ever beaten me in a race?" Joses asked rhetorically as he playfully smacked Cleopas on the back of the head.

"Good point, brother. I guess that's why they call me, 'the Turtle,'" Cleopas admitted in an apologetic, self-deprecating way.

"No worries," Joses assured his older brother as he looked at Jonathan and Jesus. "All in good fun."

The men continued walking toward the village now less than five hundred cubits away.

Pointing to Jesus, Cleopas explained to Joses, "This man has journeyed with us all the way from Jerusalem. He is a great Teacher. It has been amazing. He has shown us the Christ in all of the Scriptures."

This clearly intrigued Joses. "Tell them something more, Teacher, so that I also can see the Christ in the Scriptures," Joses pleaded curiously.

Jesus began. "When we ended our last discussion, we considered the genealogy of Christ and how it flowed through Zerubbabel, who lived five hundred years before Christ and, thus, portrayed His lineage up until the very end of the events in the Tanakh."

"How long ago was it that the very final events in the Tanakh took place?" Joses inquired.

"The final events recorded in the Scriptures took place about four hundred years ago, as seen in the life and ministry of Nehemiah. In fact, Nehemiah is a type of Christ. A 'type,' Joses, is a historical fact that illustrates or points to a spiritual truth. In general, Nehemiah's work reflects the restorative ministry of Christ. More specifically, Nehemiah points to the attitude of the Son of God[8] in that he gave up his high position in order to identify with and serve the people.[9] Like Christ, he comes to Jerusalem with a specific mission and completes it.[10] Consistent with the Christ as well, Nehemiah's life was marked by prayerful dependence on God.[11] In these ways, in the Tanakh, Nehemiah points to the coming Messiah."

"That is amazing," Joses remarked as he was clearly still meditating on the things Jesus had just said. "It has been said that the Christ is God. He is eternal. Do the Scriptures paint this picture?"

Jesus bent over and began drawing in the dirt again, almost as if to also give Joses the "classroom" experience to which Cleopas and Jonathan had become accustomed.

"Nathan prophesied concerning the interaction between God the Father and God the Son, 'I will establish his throne forever. I will be his father and he shall be My son[12]; and I will not take My lovingkindness away from him, as I took it from him who was before you. But I will settle him in My house and in My kingdom forever, and his throne shall be established forever.'[13] Surely, the eternality of the Son of God is seen in the Scriptures."

Just then, they approached the village and the path that led to Cleopas' house. Jesus continued walking on the road as though he were going to continue His journey.

---

8   Philippians 2:5-7
9   Nehemiah 1:11; 2:11-18
10   Nehemiah 2:5; 6:15
11   Nehemiah 2:4; Nehemiah 4:9; Matthew 26:39-44; John 5:19
12   Hebrews 1:5
13   1 Chronicles 17:12-14

"Teacher," beseeched Cleopas, "stay with us. It is nearly evening, and it will be dark soon."

So, Jesus followed them to the house and went in to stay with them. As they reclined at the table, Jesus introduced His final point about how He is seen in the Scriptures.

"Let me ask you again. What is the single most miraculous event in all of history?"

"You told us, Teacher," affirmed Jonathan. "It is the incarnation of God. It is the Son of God becoming a Man."

Jesus nodded His head. "You are a good student, Jonathan."

Jesus continued. "Solomon prophesies of the incarnation. 'But will God indeed dwell with mankind on the earth?'[14] Here he is speaking about the inadequacy of the temple to be a space in which God could dwell."

"Well, that is true," confirmed Cleopas. "How can the fullness of God dwell on earth?"

"Ah." Jesus nodded. "This is the miracle of the incarnation; that God Himself dwells on the earth. Jesus is this miraculous temple. 'For in Him all the fullness of Deity dwells in bodily form.'[15] In referring to Himself, Jesus says, 'Something greater than the temple is here.'[16] God did dwell in the temple in the Old Covenant, but, now He dwells among us more perfectly in His Son. Even as the new is not different from the old but only more perfect, complete, and revealing, so, too, the God of the New is not a different God than the God of the Old but only a more perfectly revealed God. Thus, in the Tanakh, you have seen pictures, types, descriptions, and prophecies all pointing to the God who would come, but now you see Him just as He is."

* * *

So one has to wonder, why didn't they see Him yet? Why did they not recognize Him? Why did Mary not recognize Him at the tomb earlier that

14   2 Chronicles 6:18
15   Colossians 2:9; Hebrews 1:3; John 1:1, 14, 18
16   Matthew 12:6

morning? Perhaps it has something to do with the fact that 'He appeared in a different form.'[17] Perhaps, someone might say, 'How are the dead raised? And with what kind of body do they come?'[18] Perhaps, then, someone might answer, 'it is sown a natural body, it is raised a spiritual body. If there is a natural body, there is also a spiritual body.'[19] The natural or fleshly body is such that the body is primary; the spirit is seen through first seeing the body; the intangible is only recognized as it is seen through the tangible. The spiritual body is such that the spirit is primary; the body is seen through first seeing the spirit, the tangible is only recognized as it is seen through the intangible.

Initially, Mary did not recognize Jesus at the tomb. But once they started conversing and He called her by name—a relational, spiritual interaction—she immediately recognized Him. Could it be that she saw His Spirit, and so, then, she saw His body?

If so, how will Cleopas and Jonathan finally recognize Jesus? Perhaps they will see Him in the context of a relational, spiritual interaction like the breaking of bread.

* * *

Jesus continued commenting on the wonder of the incarnation. "And yet, this miracle concerning how and where God dwells becomes even more mysterious.[20] Do you not know, Cleopas, that you are a temple of God? And do you not know, Jonathan, that the Spirit of God dwells in you?"[21]

"How can this be?" Jonathan probed.

"Do you not remember," Jesus explained, "how He said that if He was resurrected and ascended, He would send the Spirit?[22] Christ will now live in you.[23] You will become the body of Christ.[24] God will now dwell on the earth

---

17 Mark 16:12
18 1 Corinthians 15:35
19 1 Corinthians 15:44
20 Ephesians 5:32
21 1 Corinthians 3:16
22 John 16:7
23 Galatians 2:20; Colossians 1:27
24 1 Corinthians 12:27; 10:16-17; Romans 12:5

through you; indeed, 'if the Spirit of Him who raised Jesus from the dead dwells in you, He who raised Christ Jesus from the dead will also give life to your mortal bodies through His Spirit who dwells in you.'"[25]

Cleopas was busy processing what was just said. He looked up at Jesus and affirmed, "This idea of Christ dwelling in us is a great mystery."

"Maybe so," Jesus said softly, "but mysteries exist so that they might be revealed."

Jesus looked at them lovingly. "Perhaps there is another mystery sitting right across from you."

Jesus 'took the bread and blessed it, and breaking it, He began giving it to them.'[26]

Suddenly, their eyes were opened, and they recognized Him. Cleopas turned to Jonathan. With his eyes almost popping out of his head, he exclaimed, "It is Him! It is Christ! It is Jesus!"

Jonathan countered, "How could we not have recognized Him when He was walking with us on the road and explaining the Scriptures to us?"

"Were not our hearts burning within us the entire time?" Cleopas rationalized. "He is risen!"

"He is risen, indeed," Jonathan proclaimed as he took Cleopas by the shoulders and shook him in a gesture of unity and celebration.

They both turned around to give their attention once again to Jesus. He was gone! He had simply vanished from their sight.[27]

"We must leave right now and return to Jerusalem," Jonathan asserted with a sense of urgency.

"Yes," added Cleopas, "we must go and report to the brethren what we have seen. We have seen Him in the Scriptures, and now we have seen Him face to face. "

Then they both shouted together, "He is alive!"

---

25   Romans 8:11
26   Luke 24:30
27   Luke 24:31

CONCLUSION

As the writer of Hebrews explains, the New Covenant is a better covenant.[1] It is better in the same sense that a refurbished house is better than the pre-refurbished house. It is the same house. It is just that the presentation or the appearance of that house has improved. It has advanced, and yet, it is still the same house. God's plan has always been the same. Man needs, and God provides. That is the Gospel. That is the Good News. What man could not achieve in order to secure his forgiveness, God did. The content of this soteriology is the same from the beginning. It does not change; only the degree of revelation of that content changes. Even as a lamb is a lesser revelation of God's provision than the Lamb, it is still the same contents— man needs, and God provides. In the lesser, yet same, revelation of the Old Testament, God's provision is seen in the sacrificial lamb, while in the greater, yet same, revelation of the New Testament, God's provision is seen in Himself, "the Lamb of God Who takes away the sin of the world."[2]

In either case—or in any case—there is a problem, and thus, there is a solution. There is a need, and thus, there is a provision. There is an inability, and thus, there is an ability. There is a failure, and thus, there is a victory. There is a sickness, and thus, there is a medicine. There is the poor in spirit, and thus, there is the kingdom. There is not a placement, and thus, there is a replacement. There is no performance, and thus, there is a substitute. There is a decrease, and thus, there is an increase. There is an emptiness, and thus,

1   Hebrews 7:22; 8:6
2   John 1:19

there is a filling. There is being lost, and thus, there is being found. There is a debt, and thus, there is a payment. There is confessing and repenting, and thus, there is receiving and embracing. There is sin, and thus, there is the cross. This is the Gospel. This is the Good News. I cannot do it, but He can. I cannot get to Him, so He came to me. And so, my response to all of this must be faith. I must believe that I am needy and that God is willing and able to provide. I must believe that His payment satisfies my debt.

How does somebody get saved? By believing and trusting in God's provision and, therefore, turning away from self and turning (repenting) to Him. Salvation is in Jesus, which means "God saves." This is how Abraham gained righteousness. He confessed his inability and believed in God's ability.[3] This is the same way people get saved four thousand years later. How is it that people get saved now? By confessing (I need God) and believing (God provides); they are saved by Jesus, or "God saves."[4] There are no "two different God's" or "two different ways to get saved." There is only one God. He is revealed to us in Jesus. There is only one way to be saved; Jesus, or "God saves," is that way. And so, it is not surprising that Jesus explained to the two disciples on the road to Emmaus "the things concerning Himself in all the Scriptures."[5] May our minds, like theirs, be opened "to understand the Scriptures."[6]

Understanding the Scriptures in this way builds our faith. We see the eternal plan of God played out over thousands of years. It is not just coincidence that God's revelation of Himself and His plan is consistent throughout His Story; it is not a history of chance; it is a history of Divine Sovereignty. In *Conversations on the Road to Emmaus,* there are over two hundred separate accounts referenced in the Old Testament that clearly reflect on, point to, predict, or describe Jesus Christ and His ministry. Every book of the Old Testament is represented. He is in "all the Scriptures."[7]

---

3   Genesis 15:1-6
4   Romans 10:9-10
5   Luke 24:27
6   Luke 24:45
7   Luke 24:27

The statistical odds of all these prophecies coming to pass in any one individual throughout the history of the world are astronomical. Dr. Peter Stoner, professor emeritus of science at Westmont College in 1953, famously calculated the odds of even just eight prophecies being fulfilled by accident. The probability was so astronomical—not to mention the odds for hundreds of prophecies being fulfilled—that an accidental/coincidental explanation would stand as utterly irrational and illogical. When grappling with this reality, it would truly be more difficult to believe in the god of chance than to simply believe in the God of the Bible.

And so, we come to the conclusion of our quest. A quest not so much to predict what was said verbatim in the conversations Jesus had with the two disciples on the road to Emmaus, but a quest to see Jesus in the Old Testament—a quest to search the Scriptures so as to search for and seek *Him* in order to please Him: "And without faith it is impossible to please Him, for he who comes to God must believe that He is and that He is a rewarder of those who seek Him."[8]

Would it be that we could say along with Cleopas and Jonathan, "Were not our hearts burning within us while He was speaking to us on the road, while He was explaining the Scriptures to us?"[9] And then would it be that He would say to us, "These are My words which I spoke to you while I was still with you, that all things which are written about Me in the Law of Moses and the Prophets and the Psalms must be fulfilled."[10] And then may our reward be that He would open our "minds to understand the Scriptures."[11]

The ultimate goal of all of this is that we would be transformed into His image, that we would know Him and be changed. This, of course, is what we are doing here. This is what the Scriptures do. They reveal Him. Revelation is life. When He opens our eyes so that we see Christ, we are changed because we see Him just as He is.

---

8   Hebrews 11:6
9   Luke 24:32
10   Luke 24:44
11   Luke 24:45

I thank God that even while writing this book, I experienced these things time and time again. Often, I would just have to "put down the pen" and begin praising and worshipping Him. I would just sit in a state of awe as waves of revelation flowed over me. As I saw Jesus more clearly in the Scriptures, I felt my faith being built up, and I sensed the transformational effect that had on me.

This is my prayer for you as well. Oh, Lord, let us see Jesus just as He is! Let our hearts burn within us. Let us see the Word of God. Let us be like Him!

> "See how great a love the Father has bestowed on us, that we would be called children of God; and such we are. For this reason the world does not know us, because it did not know Him. Beloved, now we are children of God, and it has not appeared as yet what we will be. We know that when He appears, we will be like Him, because we will see Him just as He is."[12]

---

12   1 John 3:1-2

ABOUT THE AUTHOR

John has spent most of his life teaching the Bible. He has taught at all levels academically, including middle school, high school, undergraduate, graduate, and doctoral levels. He has served on numerous college faculties, including Oral Roberts University, Geneva College (CUTS Philadelphia), Tidewater Bible College (Bible Teachers Institute), and Bethel College. As an international Bible teacher, John has ministered on five continents in over twenty countries. He is the author of MOTMOT (a two-thousand-page series of teaching curriculum designed to equip Bible teachers, consisting of forty-nine courses, covering six major areas of study, totaling seven hundred hours of teaching material, available in ten languages, and used domestically and internationally). His ministry has also included the founding of multiple Bible institutes as well as a missions organization, the planting of churches, and a variety of pastoral roles in the local church.

John's greatest blessing is his wife Audrey and their six children and their families. His most loved hobby is anything to do with the "beautiful game," the game of soccer. John played Division I soccer at the University of Delaware in the early 1980s. He still plays, although at a much slower pace, and coaches at a variety of levels most notably being awarded multiple times with the Coach of the Year award for his work with his varsity high school team. John loves to have fun and, as one of his grandchildren says, joke around. This, perhaps, still goes back to his days as an improvisational comedian in the network television comedy troupe, the L.A. Connection!

Dr. Mannion currently serves as senior associate pastor of True North Church and president of True North College. He holds the Doctor of Ministry (D.Min.) degree from Reformed Theological Seminary. His most recently published work is the devotional *Nuggets of Truth: A Bible Student's Devotional and a Bible Teacher's Resource Handbook.*

ALSO BY
DR. JOHN MANNION . . .

Nuggets

of truth

A BIBLE STUDENT'S DEVOTIONAL

and

A BIBLE TEACHER'S
RESOURCE HANDBOOK

DR. JOHN MANNION

Inspirational writing meets Bible commentary, *Nuggets of Truth* stands as a different kind of devotional. It is, perhaps, more in keeping with Oswald Chamber's *My Utmost for His Highest* in that it is meant to teach more than it is meant to simply inspire. Not that each Nugget of Truth does not inspire. On the contrary, it stands as a very inspirational book even as the Scriptures themselves never fail to inspire. Indeed, the content of each individual devotional is full of Scripture. Each Nugget of Truth is designed to provide the reader with a short Bible study. Hence, the reader is more of a student than simply a reader. The considerable content of each day's study digs deep enough with a pointed focus that the student effectively goes through a mini Bible college program once having gone through the entire year.

The sub-title of *Nuggets of Truth, A Bible Student's Devotional and A Bible Teacher's Resource Handbook*, reveals the two-fold purpose and use of this book. It is meant to be a devotional for Bible students and for Bible teachers. In keeping with this second purpose, the devotional is exhaustively indexed. With its indexes, Nuggets of Truth can be used by Bible teachers as a resource for their teaching ministries.

Eighty pages of downloadable indices available with purchase!

Available from your favorite retailer

For more information about

Dr. John Mannion
and
Conversations on the Road to Emmaus
please visit:

www.bibleschoolforthenations.com

Ambassador International's mission is to magnify the Lord Jesus Christ and promote His Gospel through the written word.

We believe through the publication of Christian literature, Jesus Christ and His Word will be exalted, believers will be strengthened in their walk with Him, and the lost will be directed to Jesus Christ as the only way of salvation.

For more information about
AMBASSADOR INTERNATIONAL
please visit:

www.ambassador-international.com
@AmbassadorIntl
www.facebook.com/AmbassadorIntl

Thank you for reading this book. Please consider leaving us a review on your social media, favorite retailer's website, Goodreads or Bookbub, or our website.

More from Ambassador International

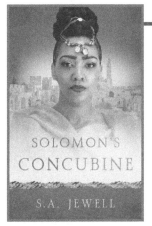

Nalussa is a simple Jewish girl, living with her family in a small town a day's travel from Solomon's kingdom. When a strange man meets her one day at the town well, Nalussa suddenly finds herself whisked away from all that she wants and desires to fulfill the lusts of a king she has never met. In *Solomon's Concubine*, S.A. Jewell uses historical references and Scripture to dive into a deeper part of Solomon's kingdom and show how God is always faithful, even when we may doubt His plan.

Terry Thompson brings the book of Daniel to life with extensive research into the lives and customs of the Hebrew people, and he even opens up the discussion for the prophecies that have yet to be fulfilled. This book is a complement to an intensive study on Daniel and the God Who is still faithful to protect His people.

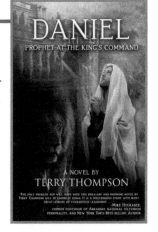

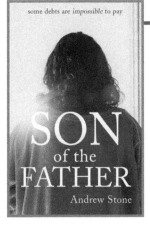

In this thought-provoking and gripping novel by debut author Andrew Stone, readers will discover a much deeper meaning as the lives of c and Jesus intertwine between the pages and weave a story of love and sacrifice.

CPSIA information can be obtained
at www.ICGtesting.com
Printed in the USA
BVHW041206240122
627024BV00015B/323